Being A Writer

What Does it Take to be a Writer?
Can Anyone Take Up the Passion

notionpress
.com

Being A Writer

What Does it Take to be a Writer?
Can Anyone Take Up the Passion

SUBHAM BANIK

notionpress.com

Notion Press

Old No. 38, New No. 6,

McNichols Road, Chetpet,

Chennai - 600 031

First Published by Notion Press 2015

ISBN: 978-93-5206-124-2

This book is dedicated to all of those people who inspired me to write, the ones who recognized my taste in writing

Thank you all

PREFACE

The book as a pretext was written on the context based totally upon fiction. It takes up references about a fictional Mumbai and its outlooks. This book was truly inspired from a Hollywood movie based upon a guy who has lost everything and is nowhere in his life. It also takes up few perspectives of our Indian society which beholds the fallen and upholds the stupid. The story is about a man, who was once an international bestseller and even won numerous awards but due to his constant personal stress leads to his downfall. It tries to bring out the situation a man sees when he sees no direction and seeks God's help. Even though, he is atheist but that does not shadow the fact that people often seek a higher power just to believe for one moment. This story is not about someone and is totally fictional. Some of the elements of Mumbai are put there as a fictional city, not on the real one even though real names are mentioned. It's not like everyone can write a story and there's a saying that 'Rome wasn't built in a day' and it's true because good things happen to those who are passionate about what they do and whatever you do you have to face hurdles and you have to overcome. I am not trying to disappoint anyone who is trying to pursue his dream but I am just trying to say that whatever you do there's a consequence and that's what the story is about. It tries to highlight every consequence our protagonist has on his every step. As for me, I am a 19 year old who is pursuing his degree in Engineering at University of Engineering and Management, Jaipur Rajasthan. I simply had the hobby of writing and wrote numerous short stories of my own. I love writing about people because I believe every person has a story, a unique story which needs to be shared, a story which needs to be told. I firmly believe that no one is boring because if a person has the ability to make a stand, he truly is a hero of his story. Everyone is a protagonist with twists and turns known as life and he should live his life to his fullest. Just a little heads up, I hope you don't get offended by the language here because if you do, I don't think you should read it. You should pick up the next pink strip.

Last but not the least, it's a give or take story

Happy Reading

Subham

ACKNOWLEDGEMENTS

A good thing cannot come out without support, even if it's for Mark Zuckerberg. So I would first like to thank my publisher Notionpress.com, without whom this story would have ever reached you. And I would also like to thank the inspirations that I got by watching too many English flicks and documentaries. I would also like to thank Barath and all of those people who supported me through my writing process. I would also like to thank MS-Word for deliberately easy typing process for making everything as easy as possible. Last but not the least, I would like to thank my family: – Mom, Dad and my sister for supporting me to write this book and who were the first people to recognize my hand in writing. Also thank you all readers for reading the book. Thank you all

P.S:- Thank You God for making me realize what it feels to do something you love

Prologue

I couldn't even remember the shit went down that night, It was like a big gloom stash of chills with onion leaves where people close their eyes just to get a momentary touch. Irony for me cause I am not the guy who usually fall for hangoverness. But still on the contrary, it wasn't always like to get high and use lemon peels the next day. Tonight was different, because neither Karan showed up nor the asshole on the next door. Tonight was the night when I finally decided to commit suicide. Seriously because people neither care to look for the books I have written nor they remember about the Pulitzer I brought to this country a few years back taking the toll up. I was drinking heavily because on the contrary, I wasn't going to get laid neither I was going to get any inspiration.

"Drinks are on me people" I shouted. Everybody yahooed

I was drinking tequila along with a booting shot upwards and then using lime to get off the madness to try once more. It wasn't usually that I get crazy but because I had already decided to kill myself, why not have a massive party before going to grave.

"Dude, you gotta stop" someone said from behind, seeing me with a vodka and two shots of tequila going down.

"Why the fuck should I stop?" I was drunk by this time and I didn't cared who was behind me.

"You know I would like to have a solitary moment so can you just fucking leave me alone" I said, cheers in the air.

Everybody returned.

"Jesus, you're an asshole" Said that someone from behind

I turned back

"Hey, nobody calls me asshole unless it's me" I said, seeing at a well-built man with a girl

"Oh yeah, what you gonna do, Grandpa?" He smirked and everyone awed

"Don't play that card man. You're not in a good position" I said, trying to remind myself of the consequences but in vain

"C'mon old man" He started laughing and everyone started to crowd the bar table

I somehow came back to my senses, atleast that's what I thought.

"Look man. I don't wanna fight okay" I said, trying to calm things down

"Why? Cause you're such a pussy" He said. Okay, he touched the line

I sighed but he didn't stop. Maybe because he was showing off in front of his girl

"You're such a pussy you need a dick to feel in"

Okay, that's it. I punched him straight in the nose. He fell down and started bleeding.

Next thing you know, there was chaos and the last thing I could hear was the bells of a temple or rather I should say my alarm and all I could see was the shoe under the bed.

Contents

1. What Happened?

Lying down on the floor of my apartment building, thinking about stars or maybe women. Looking at the old cassette tape which got wasted last night due to my rendezvous and angry approach. Life took a different turn and the moment you think 'you can't do it' is when life gives you disastrous things to remember till you take it to the grave. Life isn't short not like the ones people usually say but for me life's a bitch. Karma, to be precise. Thinking about the times when I sinned just for the benefit of doubt. When I look back in time at what I used to be and what I have become now, it is like thinking about serious crap. Well, keeping those things aside, I struggle to get myself up after last night's hangover. Scratching my eyes, sitting idle with my mouth open and recalling in my mind everything that happened till now. I used to be a respectable guy back in the days but when things happen, people no longer see you as a comfort zone; they usually prefer to see you as the next douche bag. I wasn't that guy, but life happened. Looking at the clock, 9:15, biting the lower tip of my lip, getting up to drink some lemonade because that's how you get over a hangover. Scratching the mucus out of the nose and seeing some bills on the table which I think needed to be paid this weekend but eyes were still dizzy. Sipping water and a serious knock on the door broke off my chain of thought. Yawning and trying to keep my eyes open, I went over to answer the door. It was Karan, or simply 'chutiya' (jackass). Officially this guy is my agent and unofficially this guy is a dick. Not to mention but we are hard-core drinking partners staying up late Saturday night just to get high from marijuana and some magic moments. He is around 35, well-educated (still drinks), comes from a good family in Pune (still drinks) and has always a commitment issue to Darshana or should we say they have an on-off relationship. For once he is seeing me in an awful condition rather than him getting into it. Tossing me the paper, he went over to check the bills and then sat on the couch, maybe wondering how to start the conversation because we already know how it will end. But this time the guy had some news to share.

"Dude, you look awful."

Frustrated I said, "Umm I know, tell me something new."

Looking up and down at my condition, he said nothing but just passed me a small paper with something written on it.

"Tell Sid that the deal is off unless he turns up with a manuscript on my desk within 12 hours and tell him I don't give a damn about his career."

I was shocked and obviously angry and stared at Karan.

He knew the situation and breathed a sigh and took the paper.

"Last night when I was about to watch the game, she was quite angry and said she couldn't reach you"

"Fuck that bitch"

Picking up the shirt and car keys, I sped off to give a piece of shit to the bitch.

The bitch is my publisher and was usually a very supportive character in my life but due to my non-response to her sexual advances, she now turns at every move to cut me down.

To me she's a socialised arrogant dick-sucking bitch but apparently the last word you cannot say to a publisher without getting fired.

It took me an hour to reach the office in Malabar Hills because of traffic jams and a whole lot of collisions to get to her office.

Storming in and the first words that came out of my mouth were:

"FUCK YOU BITCH"

The room was air-conditioned with glass doors along with two dicks sitting across from the bitch with their vendetta about possible new writers.

I didn't give a damn that moment but still a quick observation.

"Really?" said she.

"No I mean figuratively."

She went back and forth her chair and gave me an unconvincing surprised look.

"What the hell do you mean by 12 hours? Even the most successful commercial writer would kick your desperate ass."

She gave me a smug look and took a deep breath and said casually

"Look Sid, I run a company on some investments and benefits and apparently you have given me nothing for the past 5 years apart from a blog which has now been deactivated because of constant asshole nagging. So…

Standing up she came close to me, close enough to let her assume that she was making me uncomfortable but at that moment I was so fucking angry at her that I didn't realise that she was indirectly making a move.

I pushed her back. She realised I was pissed off and she adapted to the situation very well.

The dicks suddenly came out thinking about the escalating tension between us.

Adjusting her hair and specs, Priyanka Devendkar, or as I put it 'The Bitch' started her speech. Laughingly,

"Sid, let me get everything straight, first, you're not writing anything, second you're facing a blockage which is definitely not my problem, third, you're a disgrace to my company and the readers because you know what they don't give a damn about you anymore. They just think you as the old moron writer who got lucky 5 years ago winning that Pulitzer Price but now times have changed and he is and alcoholic psychopathic son-of-a-bitch…"

"Don't you dare…"

"Oh I will you asshole, just because you've got a cute face and a golden heart doesn't mean you're a saint. You're still that killer who went to jail…"

"That was a fucking long time ago"

"Not very long"

"Come to the point"

"The point is I don't give a shit about your career, not because you didn't sleep with me but because you're no one right now and people don't give a shit of your existence"

"Oh c'mon you're really not going down that road"

"Oh yes I am, and let me further get things straight, if I don't get a manuscript on my desk within the next 2 weeks, you're out. O-U-T, Am I being clear with you?"

"Do you seriously think I can write in two weeks?"

"No I don't and in that way I don't have to go through the formality of kicking your ass out of here but I rather sue you in a court of justice"

"You can't do that because we have a deal and that takes us back to square one"

"Oh you forgot the agreement" she said, making a gesture "The deal was for 4 years and we're on year 5 and you're still at the company because of my mercy and I would have legally put your ass on the road, kicked and fucked and let me remind you, Siddarth Kumar Banerjee, DON'T YOU DARE EVER WITH ME"

She was quite angry, but kind of awkward cause the situation got reversed. Figuratively, she got my ass kicked.

Nothing more to pursue, we removed eye contact and I went out through the door.

"Just so you know, don't ever EVER show your fucking face here after 2 weeks."

I was pissed off but I had nothing to say, I just wanted to get my head out of that office. Everyone had listened to what was happening back there and kept staring at me till the elevator came.

I was nothing but a piece of shit. Sad and alone…

2. Damsel in Distress

It was evening time at Marina Drive and migratory birds were making their way home. Office workers were stuck in the traffic jam near the beach. Couples were making out, some were having sex inside the car but none of them lifted my mood. The breeze from the Arabian Sea was majestic and calm but one thing cannot make a man's day sometimes. Apparently, I think she was right. You know what I was, that was a long time ago. Success was eminent for me but the ship has sailed and now I need something concrete to get back on the market and that too within two weeks. Seriously everyone needs time and writing aint a dog's shit which you can put out at the side of the road. But apparently this is not the time for thinking about bullshit. Smoking out, I was already on my 3rd cigarette but I wasn't feeling high. It was not just a basic day like others. The phone ringing surprised me suddenly.

It was chutiya

"Hello"

"Bol be chutiye"

"Kya hua, Kya boli randi ne?"

"We had a falling out and apparently I've got two weeks to write a book."

"Damn man, total damn"

"Where the fuck are you anyway?'

"Darshana"

"Sala chudte rahega kya"

"Nah man just needed some love making"

"What's that?"

"You know when you're feeling low and need something to pass the time out"

Crap, this guy was total crap. All he could think about is sex and like it or not he even gets it.

"Chal sun, pick me up in 30 near the dhaba"

"Can't man, got some personal things to handle"

"What? To jerk off"

"Nah man, some other stuff, talk to you later"

Beep, He hung up. I would not rather talk about shit-break, I mean seriously by his crappy standards he has a lot of say in his circle of environment. Not to mention, he has a shoulder to lean upon. On the other hand, I got divorced two times, and have 3 children, 1 from the first and 2 from the second. Well usually marriage is the union of two souls together for seven births according to Hindu beliefs but I am a big disgrace to my religion too. It seems there is no way for me other than to give up. But still on one part of my brain has got some optimism that things will turn right and everything will end well. Street lights started coming on and I went off to Blueberry near the commercial Bandra. I didn't take any cabs as I wanted to walk just to enjoy the moment. At my age, people tend to settle down and plan for a retirement. I am not that old, 41, but still I get this feeling that I could've got a happy family but I screwed things up bad, big time. My ex-wives hate me, the second got married three months ago and the first is still hunting. My three kids are Rima, Sanjay and Komal. Rima's a teenager and needs guidance from time to time. Usually because she has already started smoking and neither me nor my first ex-wife Radhika could stop it. My other children love me and from time to time I bring them gifts which also make their day. They're yet to reach 10, one being 6 and the other 8. Still I love being with them. My second ex-wife Mona hates me and only sees me for the sake of the children. And somehow everything's managed until now.

Reached Blueberry, my usual drinking spot. Blueberry for me is a peaceful place but yeah most of the time young people dance and come for drinks. For me, Blueberry is somewhat like an inspiration. Most of the time I write about this place in blogs, speech and books and that's why I usually get a discount on every drink I order. People usually come here for 'ONS' or as should I put it, One-night-stand. Guys check out girls, girls browse men and the next thing you know, they're out of here. Anyways I am not a big fan of ONS because I still believe in love-making. Call me old-fashioned but I still try to be the nice guy.

"The usual, Sir?" asked Prateek, the bartender who knows what I always order, one shot of gin with a lemon peel.

"Yes, no wait bring me vodka straight up and no lemon"

"Oh ok, you want to get drunk today Sir?"

"Don't care to even mention it"

"Sure Sir"

Leaving me at the table, I started to read all the brands of the bottles kept at the shelf. Johnny walker, Magic Moments.

"Dude" someone patted me at the back and took the stool next to me. I turned to look; it was chutiya.

"Thanks, you came at a very right time" sarcasm in my voice.

"I am still with you man and I am not letting you go that easily. We can think of something, something solid and you're going to be famous again."

"For the love of God, shut up. You know it's impossible to write in 2 weeks and you're talking about fucking solid. Solid eh, this fucking table is solid; the bottles at the drawer are solid."

Prateek brought my drink and understood the situation and left us in peace.

"Look I know you're upset and I completely understand that but you can't just give up"

"Give up, seriously what the fuck are you? I am not writing for more than a year now and you're talking about understanding. Hell, I could've thought you as a friend but I think this drink is far better than you. At least it's giving me satisfaction and shutting up about it. I am fucked and you know that completely but instead I would prefer if you don't give me any crap about giving up and understanding."

I sipped my drink in one scoop and signalled Prateek for another round. He nodded.

"Let me just talk to her and maybe we can come to terms"

"Oh fuck it, I don't want to come to any terms. And she already fired me, she's just waiting for the right moment to kick my ass out."

Prateek brought the second round."I will have a beer" said chutiya.

"The point is, she wants a manuscript right, so we write some normal story and shove it up her ass."

Kind of desperate and needed the time to pass, I deliberately listened his stupid fucked idea.

"And what would be that?"sarcasm.

"You know like a boy meets girl, girl meets boy, love at first sight, climax and a happy ending."

I took a specific 9 second look at his stupid face. Seriously this guy was stupid as hell.

Prateek brought his beer.

Sipping his beer, he continued

"We will add some twist to it"

"Like"

"You know like-SEX"

"Seriously Sex"

"Yeah, the market is very strong who writes about sex like fantasization. You know like a girl comes over a boy's house and they both fuck. Ooooo, smoking hot brother"

"You mean people literally like to read about sex? Are you fucking nuts? People like the plot and characterization."

"That's what you like not the mass"

I signalled for the third round.

"Fuck you man and keep your fucking ideas to yourself"

I returned to enjoying my drink

"Sorry man, I thought you might like the idea"

"Well you guessed wrong"

Finishing my drink, I signalled for a fourth. Chutiya ordered his second beer.

"Sometimes I believe you really need to get laid"

Making a surprise gesture "Why?"

"Then you would have known what are the benefits of writing sex"

"Shut up, Just shut the fuck up"

"Honestly dude, pick up a nice girl, offer her drinks and take her home"

"I hate one-night-stands"

"This isn't ONS. You might even enjoy the company of a female counterpart"

"Dude I don't need to get laid"

"Okay, your call"

Finishing up, I ordered for tequilas

"Man, you need to stop"

"Just leave me alone"

I guess he had nothing to do but to go.

"Okay but call me in the morning, we can talk of a new idea and take it easy man."

"Yeah whatever"

Chutiya left. Leaving me all alone in the company of tequilas and my conscience.

Tequilas were flowing down my spine and I was getting drunk by every drink.

Quite right, the dumbass was. I mean yeah people like to read in what they're interested in. And apparently, ours is a big populated country where people like to fuck and He is true about the fact that who doesn't like sex. Whether manual or real, people love it. And some of the dumbass writers make money through it. Nobody likes a stupid biography about pyramids, cancer or history of Aravalli range mountains anymore. So people write love stories plus the sex because more the sex, more the sell and more the money and more the demand. Conclusion, paper or body, sex is important…

3. Lucky

"Hi there" said a pretty lady with a tight bourette dress with a cleavage. She ordered for a dirty ginger.

"Hi" couldn't finish the first set cause I didn't wanted to get drunk when I was looking at her assets.

Her upper transparent lining along with a thin necklace just suited her. And the perfect fact was that she was wearing a feathered peacock earring which just was matching to her brunette hair and her blue eyes. She had a perky nose along with small lips She had the perfect ass and the amazing boobs as her nipular area was a little visible. She was wearing a upper heel with a perfect matching black stockings. Her smile was golden as she offered me a drink. I kind of assumed she was trying to hit on me.

I was kind of flattered so I took the drink and she started the conversation. There was a piano jazz music playing in the background. Prateek brought more tequilas for both of us.

"So what do you do?"asked she

"I am a writer"

"Oh like Chetan Bhagat" she was giggling

"Ah, yeah, like him" seriously nobody heard me.

"So what stories have you written?"

"Umm mostly biographies and stuff"

"Oh" I could sense her lack of interest in this type of stuff and her disappointment in this conversation

"Boring, isn't it?"

"No, just never heard of them"

"Yeah, I guess, we are not exactly the famous type of people"

She broke into laughs. I was glad to bring a smile on her face.

"And?" she asked

"And what?"

"What else do you do?"

"Boring stuff"

"Like?"

"Cooking, Watching TV and Facebook"

"You can cook?"

"Yeah, sort of hobbies I picked up"

"Wow, that's kind of cool"

"Thanks, so what do you do?"

"Ah, you know boring stuff" she broke into giggles

"Like?"

"Dressing, sleeping Facebook and going to college"

"Oh college girl, that's cool" Shit, she's too young for me to even consider a normal handshake.

"No, sorry what?"

"What?"

"I could sense a sudden discomfort in your voice. What is it?"

"No, nothing"

"Seriously, spit it out" She was serious at that moment

This girl caught me in a dumbstruck position and I have no option left

"It's just that, I never talked to a college girl" Sigh of relief

"Oh, well I never talked to a grown up man"

At that moment, we made eye contact and smiled at each other. Kind of awkward for me.

"You know at first I thought you're kind of cute but now I realised you're honest too" she said

"Oh yeah, what made you believe that"

Sipping her drink she continued

"You know most of the guys I met they obviously had a fake reputation and overwhelmed feelings but you were honest about who you were and how you feel.'

"So you do know me"

"Seen your face somewhere maybe years back but kind of forgot your name"

"Sid Banerjee"

"Right, didn't read your books but have seen you"

I was kind of blushing at the same time happy

"Awww, you're blushing" she broke into more giggles

"Well somebody recognised me and that too not from reading the books"

"Well I would love to read them"

There was a momentary eye contact and again we both smiled at each other. We went back to our drinks and a remix track was put on the disc.

"You want some hot coffee or something?" she asked suddenly

Coffee, I thought it was not a bad idea to get some coffee and I needed some to sober myself up and I might enjoy the coffee and it's a long time when someone's offering me coffee. Friendly or what, I felt a dying need for coffee that moment.

"Yeah, coffee sure" I replied back

"Let's get out of here" and she took her purse

"I thought you were going to buy me a coffee" I said

"No, I have some stack back at my place"

"Oh okay"

"Do you have a problem with that?" she asked

"No, no, not at all"

She picked up her coat and started to walk towards the door. I paid Prateek and said to keep the change just not to wait or I might lose the opportunity of free coffee by a female. So I took off. We took a cab and she directed the cabbie to Andheri West. She was talking about her course of journalism and how she changed majors just to go through with her passion of anchoring. One thing bugged me about the coffee, I mean seriously 'Do you need to go to her place just to get a cup of coffee?' but I kept quiet assuming she might be saving money for college so she might offered coffee from her deck. She kept going about her likes and dislikes till we reached her place. I paid for the cab as she was unlocking the door. We went in and she went off to switch on the lights.

"So what's your name?" taking off my coat

"Zerifa" she replied back from one of the rooms

I sat down on the couch filled with lingerie, assuming it's a girl's apartment

"Make yourself comfortable" she said

"Okay" I replied back. Kind of awkward sitting on a couch in a girl's apartment and that too 1 hour before midnight. Remembering that I need to meet Rima the next day and to meet the kids, I waited for my host and her self-made coffee.

She brought coffee in a mug and sat next to me. The coffee was okay if you're looking for standards.

"So how's the coffee?"

"Good actually"

"Ah, I am glad, ouch! oh god"

"What happened?"

"I got a sudden ache in my shoulder"

"Let me look" putting the coffee on the table

She sat on her back and I started massaging her

"Hmm that feels good"

"Yeah?"

"Uh-huh"

"You are really beautiful"

I don't why but those words came out straight out of my mouth. Maybe thc moment might have anticipated it.

"Hmm, why do you say that?" turning back

Our lips were millimetres away from each other. I was looking at her eyes and her lips and she was doing the same.

Don't know who initiated but we kissed and we kissed for like 2 minutes after which I entered my tongue in her mouth.

It was a deliberate French kiss and took us long 10 minutes to break as people also needed air to breathe.

She started unlocking my belt and I did my shirt buttons. She started to unzip her bourette and I took off my shirt and pants.

She was naked, totally naked and I mean she was fucking beautiful. There was a small black spot on her left breast which was kind of cute. She had considerable pubic hair which was overwhelming.

We smiled at each other and came close to kiss. She put down my boxers and starting touching my dick. It kind of turned me on. I fingered her a little bit and came down to suck her amazing boobs. I took her in a lap as she laughed and took her to the bedroom. I kissed her in the neck and was going down south. She was making orgasmic noises. I reached her clit and kind of fingered her more. It turned her on. She pushed me back on the bed and started kissing me on the neck. She kissed my chest, navel and started to give me a blowjob. It was amazing, I mean the last time I got a blowjob was from Mona and that too like a year ago. I was rock solid hard at that time and was looking at her face.

"You got condoms?" asked she

"No"

"Wait"

She went over to the drawer next to the bed and took out a condom

"Here"

"You got a stock I see"

"Men usually don't bring one so…" we broke into giggles. Seriously Men were dumbass.

We both took a laugh and she took the cowboy position. I entered her and she gave an cuming noise and started riding.

It was so fucking hot, I mean like I used to hate ONS but I guess it isn't that shitty as I thought. We were riding hard and I pushed her to the bed and took the missionary position. I was pushing her hard and it was pretty fucking hot. After half an hour of pushing each other and making noises, we both came together. Oh man, cuming on a female cervix is so fucking better than doing with the hand. Shit, we don't need a tissue for it.

We were breathing hard and laughing at the same time as it was so fucking great.

"Want a cigarette?"

"Cigarette, Yeah sure"

She brought her cigarette pack from the drawer. We both lighted up.

I saw it was 10 minutes past one. She was smoking quietly. I was making smoking rings.

"You must have a hard life" she said

"Why is that?"

"You know, you always don't find a good story to write"

"Yeah maybe"

Sigh

"What about you?" I asked

"Me?"

"Yeah, like must have been hard studying as well as taking care of yourself, you know and you said you were living the dream" I smiled at her

"No, it's not like that, I mean yeah it was tough for a while but things worked out for me I guess"

"Hmm"

"Why you were so much stressed?" she said

"Stressed?"

"No one takes a vodka along with a set of shots unless he's got a whole lot of problems on his ass."

We both smiled at that reference.

"Nah it's nothing like that, it's just....none of your business"

"Well, I want to hear about it"

"Why? It's stupid"

"Well, I don't know, it might help us to pass the time till we get ready again"

I understood her signal that moment and went over to kiss her. She smiled and kissed me back.

We were laughing and kissing as I switched off the lights...

4. Responsibilities

I sometimes really missed being the nice guy. You know, the guy who usually is brought up by strict conservative parents till he reaches the age where he acquires blue films to watch naked women just to jerk off. That guy who always studies for the sake of marks and to impress the first ranked girl only to get her attention. The guy who goes to tuition, makes friends and starts to get, you know spoilt. He starts drinking by the time HS exams come and takes admission in a crappy private engineering college just for the tag of engineer to acquire. Well those are mostly nice guys and my destiny wasn't like that, I mean not totally like that, I mean some of the things were true, I mean really happened to me but I didn't go to an engineering college instead I had gone to a university to finish off my majors in Physics which landed me to nothing. At one point, I thought about PhD but concentration is not my middle name and studies aren't my thing so I left it. Felt something in writing, so gave it a shot and got 3 books published where one of them got the prestigious Pulitzer Price. Didn't thought about deserving that award but still maybe the jury liked my book so voted for me, I guess. Those were the days of fame and I honestly liked it. Women were totally on me and it was like sex, booze and awesomeness but guess paradise has sailed to a new harbour and I landed in two divorces, alimony, children and I am almost broke. I was thinking all of this while looking at the ceiling of the apartment of the girl I fucked last night. The apartment was okay and I guess she paid her rent. Saw some stockings of clothes here and there and so that rules out tidiness. Saw cute show-pieces, guessed she loved art and maybe some sand painting cause a beautiful one with the woman carrying her child was hanging on the wall. An ashtray was near the lamp table and I remember she keeps cigarettes on the drawer. Pulling out a one and lighting it, I tried to plan out what I needed to do that particular day. She was asleep and was perfectly beautiful. I could see her sideboob against her pillow and kind of wanted to suck cause they were so perfect last night. She suddenly yawned ruining my chain of thought.

Looking at me woke up with a cigarette

"In the morning? Seriously?" she was shocked and surprised

"Felt like it" I replied

She saw the clock on the wall, 7:30.

"Shit" she hurriedly got off from the bed and reached for her panties and bra.

"What happened?" Puffing out a smoke

"I have college" she panicked "Shit" she took her bourette and took off to change.

I was smiling and smoking, kind of creepy doing both together

But it was really awkward that moment cause it was a long time that I got laid. The last time I had sex was with Mona before we were married. I got off from the bed and started getting dressed. My cell was ringing and it was Rima. Fuck, forgot that I needed to meet her in 8:30 at my house. I dressed quickly and was going out.

"You going?" she asked, I sensed a little bit of surprise as well as disappointment.

She was dressed in a uniform and was smelling beautiful as if like she got out of bath right now.

"Yeah, forgot that I need to meet a client" I lied

"Okay, be sure to call me"

"Yeah, sure"

I got out of her house as soon as possible. 'Call me' yeah right girl I didn't even took your number. I will sure to remember that. Took a cab from there to my house. I already saw Rima at the entrance sitting and texting on her Smartphone. She brought a bag with her, probably her mother had sent her to me in the hope of keeping her for at least 2 days. I paid the cab and went over to unlock the door. She saw me and went back to her texting. We entered the house and she went to sit on the bed. I took a bottle to quench my thirst. She was looking at me straight in the eyes.

"Where were you last night?" asked she

"Working" I replied back

"Say it"

"What?"

"That you're drinking"

"No I wasn't" I tried to lie but she was already staring at me, probably convinced by her deduction.

"Ok I was, does it matter?"

"It matters to me"

"Why?"

"Uh, cause you're my Dad"

I tried to make a gesture at her response but couldn't. It wasn't to act in front of kids these days, I mean they have become really smart and curious. Back then, we would have already gotten a slap by now for these questions. I tried to pass the bottle to her. She was drinking water and I was looking for a topic of conversation.

"So, how are you?" I asked

"What do you expect?" she said

"I said 'How are you', it's a simple question"

"Well apparently I don't want to answer it" she replied. She really gets on my nerves sometimes but I had to stay calm.

"Okay, alright so I am going to make some breakfast. So you want to join me?"

Staring at me "Seriously Dad, you don't know Mom, she would never allow me to go to your house without making my stomach full."

Yeah, I forgot, Radhika does that, She is really sensitive when it comes to food. I never felt hungry when we were together. Good times, I guess.

I went over to kitchen closet to look for some cereals. Found some near the rack of dishes. Went over to the refrigerator to look for Wednesday's milk. I guess 2 days earlier milk isn't really spoilt. Yeah whatever, I needed something in my empty stack so I think these two will do. Eating and cleaning the dishes and putting them back, I went over to Rima who was still busy texting.

"So how you've been?" I asked

"Fine!!" still looking at the phone

"Okay, so what do you want to do today?"

"I don't know"

"We can catch a movie since its Friday. What films are on?"

"I don't know, I am not a movie lover Dad"

Yeah I guess you're not. She was still busy at the phone which kind of angered me a little bit.

"You know you came here to spend some time with me not with that gadget" I said with a lot of patience.

She stopped midway and looked at me

"Just because we are at your house doesn't mean we need to, you can see your other children" she said

"What do you mean by that?" I asked

"You know exactly what I mean by that"

"So what are you trying to imply here that I don't care about you like I do for San and Komal" I asked with a sarcasm in my voice

"No, I am not implying that, I am saying that you can see your other children, you don't have to worry about me" she was awfully calm saying this

"No, no, but I worry about you, the same as I worry about all of my children. You're all part of me and its my duty to take care of you and love you till I breath my last."

"Well apparently I don't need your care and love, I am giving you your freedom from duty"

Okay, she was way over the line. I was breathing hard, I wasn't good with Rima, she always manages to piss me off.

"Rima, its not what you're saying, You're my daughter, I love you and I care for you and you cannot take that back from me" I angrily told her.

She was staring "I can" she said

"Rima, I want to help you and be there for you"

"So you should have thought that before marrying again"

"It was a mistake, I know I did some mistakes but I am redeeming myself for it and I need you for this" I honestly said with a much calmer voice

"I don't need you Dad. I am better off on my own with my mother. We don't need you so stop letting me be your daughter" she was yelling at me.

SLAP

She started to cry, and I was breathing hard.

"Thanks Dad, thank you very much, I swear to God I will never see you again"

She stormed off and I wasn't in a mood to catch her. She seriously was way over the line.

'Go after her' my inner voice said. I am still a father. I went out and she was sitting by the stairs crying. I tried to comfort her but she moved back. I was feeling sorry for her and angry at myself for hitting her. She is my angel and will always be. God, I loved her so much. She wanted to go home so I took my bike out to drop her at her mother's. On the way, flashbacks from her birth was starting to come in front of me as how I was happy after she was born and how we were happy together as a family and how after the divorce we got distant and still. I was crying from the inside as I wanted to get things back again with her but maybe it was my fault. I hit her and maybe I shouldn't have. She is just a kid and kids always do mistakes. I should have been with her during her growing up years but I wasn't.

We reached her mother's place and she went off to her room crying. Radhika was surprised to see me and her daughter crying.

"What happened? You hit her?" she asked

My silence was enough for her. "What is wrong with you?" she asked

"I am sorry, I just got carried away with what she said and...."

"God, you're so insane" she said

"I know" I suddenly observed she was wearing a night gown at 11 in the morning.

"You're wearing a nightie?" I asked with raised eyebrows

"Oh, umm, I forgot to change" she said

"Right" but I wasn't convinced with her answer and suddenly saw a pair of men's shoes in the welcome carpet. She quickly noticed.

"It's just the lumber fixing the pipes and the sink" she hurriedly gave me an explanation.

"Okay" she could sense I wasn't exactly satisfied with the answer.

"I have to go" she said and closed the door. Something was going on but I was pre-occupied with Rima crying that I ignored it and went to start the bike. My phone ringed and it was chutiya calling. He said to meet him at the new 'Burger King' at Oberoi in 30. I kick-started the bike and went off. The day wasn't exactly I hoped it would be.

5. Bare Beginnings

Reaching at the new Burger King in Oberoi wasn't exactly a bad idea and as chutiya likes to eat American food more than his Indian stomach can manage. There wer couples and families, all trying the new burgers along with cokes. People were in a queue to pay and take their order. I took a normal corner seat just by the window to enjoy the outside. There were laughs and love all smeared around with cheese and tissues. It was kind of funny to watch people eat and do stupid stuff at the same time. Chutiya took 15 minutes later to arrive and sat across me. He already had a menu on his hand and was looking into it for something to eat.

'Aren't you going to order?" he asked

"No, I just had breakfast, I am good" I said

"Then have lunch, these place is new and I heard it's good"

"No, I am fine"

"C'mon man, I don't want you to be that creepy guy who sits in a fancy restaurant but doesn't orders"

"Why does it matter so much? Just tell me what you have to say and I will leave"

"Seriously this attitude is a bummer man, you have to be down to earth"

"I am down to earth, What the fuck is wrong with you?" Few staring eyes were at our table because of my yelling.

"Sorry" I said

"It's okay, I was just looking out for you man"

"Okay, I will order something"

"Nah, it's cool if you don't want to order"

"What do you want me to do, order or not?"

"I want you to be cool"

"I am cool"

"Okay, alright"

There was awkward silence for 5 minutes.

"I have an idea for you" he said

"What's that?"

"I know it's going to sound crazy but I really think you should give this love thing a shot"

"What are you talking about?" I asked

"Do you remember what I said last night?"

"Yeah, that you're fucked up" I said with a sarcasm

"No, I told you to write about love and sex thing, worth while by giving it a shot"

"Well apparently I already told you my answer I bet"

"Yeah you did, but seriously man, you need to consider it and these might get your reputation back"

Come to think of it, at some point he was right. I just can't back anymore, I really need something to get back. Something that will make people read my books again.

"Okay, but I don't know how to write love stories and shit" I said

"Yeah and I am going to help you cause I have a lot of pending ideas ready to squash out"

"Okay, I will catch you later" I said

"No, I am going to call you and make yourself free this afternoon"

"Got it"

I took off from the restaurant, was hungry but it didn't mattered that time as I seriously need to do some research on this love shit as I decided that I am going to write about it after all. Things, places and women. Everything from A to Z. I need to decide the moment, the connection and the chemistry as I got no time and it's already Friday and I got like 13 days to complete this shit. I went to the nearby book store in Santa Cruz. Got some few love novels written by some of the best writers of our country, according to the shopkeeper. Went to the wine store to get some beers and got home. My house needed renovation but it's not the best time to discuss about other stuff.

I switched on my laptop and opened MS-Word. Picked up a book and read the first and second chapter. The writer was good and I mean the depth he mentioned about his feelings was amazing but it wasn't a time to judge. I start to pander on word and only got the title.

'A CRAZY THING CALLED LOVE'

I liked the title, keeping in mind about the love thing and starting with a phrase about that a guy was struggling in life. I was hoping about a twist which wasn't exactly up to the mark. My resolve broke down way faster than a ice melts to liquid. I was pressing my forehead, depressed that I couldn't write anymore, started to feel bad about myself and thinking about giving up. Suddenly a knock on the door startled me and I went over to answer it.

"Hey" said chutiya. I looked at the clock and it was 130.

"You are already on course" said chutiya after looking my laptop open.

"I broke down" I said

"What?"

"I can't write anymore" I said with a sigh and sat down on the couch.

"Dude, you can't give up, you can't let that bitch win, you're writer and you'll always be and no matter how tough it is there is always a story, remember that you told me, that's how I got into this shit"

He was hoping for a response but I was occupied with stuffs. I mean, literally I am a gone asshole. I don't have any knowledge to give anymore but he wanted a response back. I took a deep breath and sipped my saliva.

"I know but I feel like I am over and there's no future for me" I said with great calmness.

"That's why I am here to help you, I so want you back on the game and kick her sorry ass"

"Yeah"

Alright, he was right. It's time to kick her ass. He hi-fived and got back to my laptop. He was giving me mental notes about a guy who moved from Assam to Delhi for better opportunities and met a girl by chance. This guy is truly like my brother and seriously trying to help me. I took a deep breath and went back to write a goddamn guy naming Suresh who falls in love at first sight with Kiran, no, too classy, falls in love with Mahi, too filmy, falls in love with Rekha, shit, that's the bollywood actress. I don't want people to picture Rekha while they were reading. Still, the name, yes it should be Niharika, a customary Indian name.

After four hours of writing shit about his first love with constant 15 pages. We took a break. Literally writing shit isn't easy always and people needed oxygen. And writing about love without feeling it is like making a Dal-Makhani without Dal. So we were writing every bit of experience that happens when you fall for the first time in our language. Not totally my language but we used customary English words like 'sophisticated, vulnerable, nostalgic' etc. Didn't want to go with complex so we kept as simpler as possible. Still I was thinking that it was total shit because half of them weren't even true. But I guess people loved crazy shit like love and marriage.

"What about his family?" I asked

"Who cares?" he said

"Well I do"

"Well you're not the one who is going to read"

"Yeah I will"

"No you won't and anyways you want the target to be happy right?" he askcd

"Who's the target?"

"People with money"

"Yeah"

"So follow the crowd"

6. No Choice

No choice I guess and I needed a story, no matter how desperate I was.

It was 8 in the morning. Beer bottles and used weed were lying here and there. The apartment was a complete mess. And my eyes were holding me up, keeping me still. Last night was fucked up. I mean after 4 hours of writing, we never got back to Suresh Yadav, the protagonist in my shit love story. We opened beer bottles, made joints and started smoking them along with drinking beer. I mean we were literally on cloud nine and were toasting to the good times. But didn't realised when the fuck did we passed out and now it's Saturday morning. Two days have gone in my 2 weeks time to write and I am still shitting around. Karan was lying on the floor with a half empty beer bottle in his hand. He was still passed out. Usually this type of things we do on a Saturday night along with a EPL game on. But yesterday was different, I mean we needed to celebrate my writing after 5 years even if it means only 15 pages. It's tough to write because it is tough to imagine and being a writer isn't an easy shit.

"Hey fucker, wake up" I kicked his hairy ass

"Hmmm" he said

"Dude, I am going to kick your balls if you don't wake up"

He woke up instantly; he knew I was damn serious

I went to the sink to wash my face. He was slapping himself trying to get over the hangover.

"Dude" with a sigh "I got to go, see you later"

"What?" I asked

"It's nothing"

"C'mon tell me"

"It's just…I forgot to tell Darshana that I have crashed at your place last night"

"Does it matter?"

"It does to her…she often gets worried"

"Well just tell her, it's not a big deal"

"Yeah it is"

"You often passed out here, and apparently she understood"

"Well this time it's different"

"How?" I asked

"Yesterday when I called you we had a big fight and apparently I told her many awful things…."

"So, couples have fights, just tell her you're sorry and everything's going to work out"

"I even told her that I will fuck some random girl and not return home"

Whoa, that's a tricky and they had a major fight but seriously chutiya, you are way over the line. She's going to leave you.

"Man, who the fuck says that" I said

"Well I did"

"You stupid ass"

"I know"

"God you asshole"

"I know I am"

"What the fuck are you waiting for? Call her"

"Yeah, yeah" he said and went out to call her.

That's why he was so fucking energetic yesterday in making me write because he wanted to spend the night somewhere just to prove his point. Seriously, guys are sometimes are so much dickheads they don't even realise what the fuck they have done and by the time they do, the ship has already sailed. That's what happened with me. He came back.

"She is not picking up" he said

"GO" I yelled at him as he understood the reference. I would never leave a shoulder to lean on-ever. I did some mistakes which ended up in two marriages but I am not going to screw up if God gives me a third chance. No, I am not.

My phone suddenly beeped. It was Radhika and she wanted us to meet and talk. I called her.

"Hello?" she said

"What do you want to talk about?" I asked

"It's about yesterday"

"What about it?"

"I think i owe you an explanation for whatever happened"

She was talking about her in a night gown and the men's shoes on the mat outside her door yesterday. But seriously I didn't cared.

"Okay" I said

"Can we meet?"

"Meet? Umm, I got some work to do so..." I said. I don't know but I wanted to avoid this as much as possible.

"Umm can you come over?" she asked. She seriously wanted to talk to me. What is wrong with her. But she is also my daughter's mother so I couldn't refuse her offer.

"In that way you can see your daughter too" she continued

Sigh "Okay, give me an hour to be there" I said

"Cool" She hung up.

If she is seeing someone that's fine by me as I don't care about her anymore. But she wanted to explain so maybe I should give her a chance. I picked up my bike keys and went off to her house but not before breakfast as I was damn hungry. I managed a Bada pao from a dhaba and took off. Took me about 15 minutes to reach her place. I rang the doorbell. She was wearing a yellow sari which was making her gorgeous. She invited me in and we both sat on the couch. She went to bring me some water. But instead she brought some biscuits, cashews and tea. It was like a normal morning breakfast in front of me. We both ate quietly and I put down the cup back to the plate after finishing. She took the things back to the kitchen. She sat down across me on returning.

"How are you?" she asked

"I am good"

"Right"

There was a momentary 2 minute awkward silence between us.

"So how's Rima?" I asked

"She is good but she kind of hates you even more now"

"Right"

Again awkward silence.

"So….what do you want to talk about?" I asked after like 7 minutes of awkwardness.

"I am sorry for whatever happened yesterday" she said after 2 minutes

Yesterday, what the fuck happened.

"But nothing happened yesterday" I clarified her

"I know you're thinking why I was in a night gown" she said biting her lower lip

Her sentence suddenly caught my attention. I was trying to decode what she meant. Women are the most difficult species to understand. Seriously they say something but they mean something else. I mean seriously what the fuck.

"Umm, not really" I managed to reply her back

"But I just want you to be cool with it" she said

"Cool with what exactly?" I asked

She took a deep breath and closed her eyes for a minute. I mean seriously girl, just say it.

"I am dating Suraj"

"Suraj, who exactly?" I was curious

"Remember there used to be a guy who gave art tuitions to Rima when she was 6."

Oh that guy, the sweet innocent, Suraj Nagrekar

"What the hell, you're dating your daughter's tutor?" I said with a scream in my voice.

"Sshh, not so loud, Rima doesn't know"

"She doesn't know you're dating?"

"She does, I mean she doesn't know who he really is"

"Wow, seriously wow"

"That's your reaction to my announcement?" she said with a sarcasm

"Yeah, well apparently I never fucked a person that young"

"We have only 3 years difference" she said and took the rest of the cups back to the kitchen sink.

What the fuck is going on, I mean my ex-wife cannot marry my daughter's tutor. I mean what the hell is going on. She was washing the dishes and blabbering about how Suraj is great and makes a perfect environment in the house. I was burning from inside, I mean the moment when I got to know about this Suraj, it's like the next moment I see him anywhere I am going to kill him for fucking my ex-wife who is the mother of my daughter. The same feeling that I am getting while Mona announced that she was engaged to that fucking businessman and the next thing you know, they're married. No, I am not going to let that happen. Checking her ass out, I went to the kitchen where she was cleaning the dishes. She was pretty happy about her relationship. I went close to her, too close and started brushing my penis against her ass and caressing her butts. She quickly responded by giving me a slap on the face and pushed me back and took a knife and warned me. The moment was over and I couldn't do anything but to leave and I did that. Kicking my bike, I went off, gosh I was going to lose her too.

7. Life's Fallout

I unlocked my apartment and the first thing I broke is our marriage vase which was near the bed. I was so fucking angry at her and Mona because they have already decided to move on. I know I did some mistakes but they could at least have given me a chance to redeem, but no they're so fucking hungry for men and bedding them that they forgot that they already have children. Shit man, first the book in two weeks and now this. I mean seriously I think God has taken a stand to make my life ruined. I was breaking down, I mean not like I still love her but I am still alone and all my ex-wives are getting married. On the bright side, I am going to be free from alimony. That kind of lighten the moods a little bit. I cleaned the broken vase on the floor and went to take a nap, it was Saturday but it wasn't one with being the simple day.

I woke up around 5 in the evening, took out a beer bottle from the fridge, got some nuts to go along with it. Switched on the television, was looking for some shit to look and suddenly looked at my laptop still open since last night. Got an idea to jerk off the moment so putted back the beer and the nuts and went to Pornhub.com, saw a MILF got banged by her son's friend and was feeling awesome. Seriously jerking off is the best option cause it helps you to get over the entire day shit and lets yourself loose. Cleaning out my lips with a tissue and was looking for something to eat. I had nothing to do that particular evening so went to back to Suresh Yadav for meeting the love of his love. Tried to put out some of the best situations using some bollywood flicks such as roses from the sky falling and slow music in the background when you fall for your love. It was shit, I mean literally but I had to right about them. Read some books which I bought from the store the other day and I was trying every possible angle for my characters to love each other. It was already 1 by the time I finished writing 4 pages. Nothing else and as no games were on that Saturday night so went back to sleep thinking what to do on Sunday.

Sunday was much of a low-key affair but it was the day I get to meet Sanjay and Komal. They are the best things that ever happened to me except being married to their mother but still it was kind of testosterone running and adrenaline rushing down as I get to meet them after one week as Mona doesn't let me meet them or see them in school or break down the divorce agreement. Kind of selfish on her part but still as a mother she has her nonsense duties towards her children. Went to her house on Malad to spend time with my kids.

She had bought a big house since marrying that fucking businessman who also brings them wholesale grains in black. Well apparently everything is on sale in India if you look it in black. On my way, I thought of the times we were happy together and how my non-working brought us down resulting in divorce, alimony and the next thing you know, I get to know she is getting married again and I am not invited. Felt like remorsing but the fact is that she left me, I tried but she took the final door and slammed and buried it and cemented it so that we can never go back to what we were so we hate each other but for the sake of children we try our best to see each other's faces. So I was specifically going to her house to do that.

Knocking on the door, looking at the new marigold flowers on the top of a window mesmerizing the nature and apparently the environment of the house.

She opened the door and was in a yellow kanjeevaram saree, she occasionally wore that usually when there's a wedding ceremony she is invited. The neckline was perfect and I bought her that saree when there was an old trade fair. She was in a good mood that moment.

"What's up with you?" seeing me in an old shirt that I also wore last week to her house and a jeans which I think may need some repairmen.

"Nothing" I replied back.

"There is something" she said as she was looking at my hair. I hadn't combed.

"Just stuff"

"I heard" she said and went to the kitchen

Didn't understand what she said but still as a courtesy

"What?"

"You were getting fired in 2 weeks" she said happily

What the hell. How did she know? Perhaps she might have been talking to Karan.

"Priyanka told me" she said trying to clear my confusion.

Yeah apparently, the bitch and my second ex-wife were friends back in the day and somehow it's a new way of getting my ass on fire.

"You haven't heard the whole thing" I said

"I know she told you to submit a manuscript within two weeks but you know..." she left the sentence.

"You know what exactly?" I asked with my teeth jittering

She was smiling as she was waiting for this moment like decades ago

"It's kind of impossible" she said

"Excuse me?" I said

"Leave it no, I just wanted to ask how are you but apparently I don't think it's a good time to talk"

Wow, she was quick to stop a conversation and I wasn't in a mood to explain myself to her.

"Where are the kids?" I asked, choosing to change the topic as I was there for them specifically.

"They are upstairs" she said while moving from the kitchen to her bedroom

I went up to see my kids instead of asking her where she was heading to cause it wasn't important for me anymore.

"Aren't you going ask me where I am off to?" she said

I was surprised but since I had no choice but to

"So where are you off to?" I asked with great politeness

"You know that businessman 'Mohit Virani' of the Virani Industries?" she was saying in proud

"No" I replied. How on earth am I going to know a businessman? Is she a dumbass?

"Well apparently, Santosh does and he has invited him and me for his launch of a new clothing brand"

I nodded

"There will be bollywood stars, high profile industrialists and so many reporters. So I thought i needed to be glamorous tonight" she said as she was checking her eyeliner in her hand mirror.

"So, where's your husband?" I asked

"I am going to meet him at his office as he already sent me a car to pick up"

"Okay, so all the best" I said and I sensed a little ego on her part.

Apparently she was trying very hard to show off that she is far off better with her husband than me but I totally ignored her which kind of pissed her off.

"Hope I don't see you when I return back" she said and went off. Not to polite I guess.

Didn't gave her too much attention because Sunday wasn't exactly the way it supposed to be so I too made no reactions on my part.

Seeing the kids was like my happiest moment. It felt like a natural ecosystem and I wanted to look at it forever.

"Daddy, how are you?" said Sanjay

"I am fine beta and what about you and Komal"

"He fought with me" said Komal, angry at him

"No I didn't" Sanjay said in defense.

This was looking like at one of the best plays, I mean looking at your children fight and begging for your support is one of the crave moments for any parent and I specially miss those with Rima. I seriously hope she will need me someday.

"So tell me how was your week?" I asked

This was my daily weekly routine. Every Sunday I ask them how their week went and they tell me different stories which really didn't mattered but still looking at their innocent faces made me feel wonderful.

8. Being Myself

We played and I told many stories just to scare them off a little bit but apparently it was so much fun to be with them. I really hate the day when they will come to know of the real world. Still, I can scare them off now with many irrational stories and they blindly believe them. Kind of easy. By 10,I put them to bed and told them a Cinderella story. I went back to my place after they were fast asleep.

Waking up in a Monday morning is the worst feeling. Apparently cause there used to be a time when I hated Mondays just because I had to go to work. But since quitting my job and apparently novels were in the apartment, I kind of felt bored because there was nothing to do anymore apart from writing books, reading others novels. But I wasn't in any mood to read or write. So I brushed, took a bath and went out for breakfast because most of the dhabas usually had paranthas during morning.

Paranthas were hot and tasty. My thirst for hunger was totally quenched. Paying off the manager, I thought about a possible mention of dhabas in my love-shit book.

"Siddarth?" said a female voice from behind.

I turned to look and it was the girl from the bar the other night.

"Hey, hi" totally forgetting her name

"You don't even remember me do you?' said she

"No I remember you" I said with a low voice

"Really, what's my name?"

Shit, "Umm ah umm" I was stammering

She gave a surprise wave in the air

"You men are all same" was her conclusion. I mean it wasn't totally my fault, like she hit on me and we went back to her place and yeah the sex was great but still she enjoyed it too and it wasn't like we are going to have a future together but shit it was so complicated that how the fuck can I explain this whole shit to her.

She was walking away "Hey stop" I said grabbing her hand

"Let me go" was her first response

"Okay at least let me explain" I said on my defence

She stopped and turned to look towards me with her arms crossed. Okay say something Sid anything.

"Apparently this is all new for me you know and I am not a big fan of ONS" I said, trying desperately to explain myself.

"ONS?" she asked me in confusion

"You know One Night Stands" I said

"So according to you, we had an One Night Stand. That's what you are trying to explain here" she was irritated by my explanation and apparently was starting to walk away.

"Please, No, that's not what I was trying to say" I said, still thinking what to say next

"Then what exactly are you trying to say?" she was looking at me with hope thinking I might come with a valid explanation but apparently I didn't have one and there was nothing to play but to be honest.

"I didn't call you because I forgot to take your number" I said with great honesty and politeness. But I was lying straight to her face.

"Yeah right" she didn't bought it. Shit

"It's true and I was in a little hurry that day as I went back to meet my girl"

"Your girl?" she was confused

"My daughter" I clarified

"Oh, you have a daughter?" she was curious

"Yes, I do" we were kind of off the topic that moment

"Hmmm" she said after like 2 minutes of checking me from top to bottom

"So we cool?" I said after 30 seconds

"Yeah" she said and I breathed a sigh of relief and apparently she was smiling too and that kind of made us smile at each other

"So what you have been up to?" she asked after our smiling session ended and we were walking down, apparently I was going back to my place and she was, ah giving me company.

"Nothing actually" I said

"Really, I thought that night you said you're screwed up enough that you wanted vodka and shots" she said giggling

Wow she had an awesome memory power compared to what shit I had in my skull.

"Yeah that night was rough" I said

"Yeah you were"

I laughed at her reference

"What?" she asked

"I was not talking about the sex"

"Then?" she asked

"I mean I had a rough everything that day and apparently I desperately needed to get drunk so that I could have thought about getting over a hangover rather than facing that shit"

"And what shit is that?" she asked, curious

"Does it matter?" I was trying to stop this topic

"Yes. You might feel better"

"I am okay"

"Oh" she was disappointed. Man, why would an ONS would want to know about my problem.

"You know I have to go, I have this gig going…." she said and was trying to take off

"No, stop, I'm sorry it's just….."

"What?" she was getting irritated

"I have some trust issues" not looking her in the eye

"Really?" she said. Apparently her tone turned interesting. She smiled which meant we were cool again.

We reached my apartment building by the time we stopped talking. She talked about her college fests, projects, assignments and other stuff. It was kind of a little bit off for the people because apparently nobody in our society would encourage a student talking to a elder apart from being a professor and since people knew I was stupid ass writer, some of them raised eyebrows looking at us, laughing happily. I kind of felt awkward but saw her being cool with it so I was pretending to be cool with her too. Nobody knew we slept together which kind of made me feel proud which kind of made me smile.

"Why are you smiling about?" she snapped, looking at my cheerful face

"Nothing, it's just you are so beautiful" I said, desperately trying to find words.

She blushed and put her hair back beside the ear which revealed her small jingle earrings which was matching accordingly to her sky blue salwaar kameez she was wearing that day.

"This is me" I said

"So you live here" she said

"Yeah"

Why it was feeling awkward to talk to her. I mean literally we slept together so no question about who's good in bed or whatever but still we were being shy. I had a nice reason because apparently it's a long time since I talked to a college girl and the last time I did, I ended up marrying her.

"You want to go upstairs" thinking that I had no conversation topics, better I'd showed her apartment.

"Seriously, you want to go upstairs? Don't you have anything to do apart from having sex with me" she said

Wow, I didn't knew I already started the sex conversation but okay

"No I wasn't thinking about sex right now, I thought I might show you my apartment"

"Why would I want to do that?" she asked

"Well we are right down where my apartment is standing and we can pass the time since we have nothing to talk to and apparently I can't walk with you anymore since I already reached my home"

"You don't have to walk with me if you don't want to" she said

"No, that's not what I meant" Fuck, girls are total creepy shit. Literally nobody can figure them out not even they themselves.

"Well since you want me to see your apartment, I have no harm in wasting my time here" she said with sarcasm

"No seriously you don't have to come if you don't want to" I said, putting back her words

"No, that's not what I meant" she must be thinking the same thing

"Well I got to go so…." I said

"Yeah me too" she replied

"Umm can I have your number?" I said with a meekly voice

We both laughed at how it sounded. She gave me her number and waved me goodbye. I assured her I would call her soon.

That's how our second meeting ended. Shit man, I kind of got this feeling that we might have a connection and things may start working for us but apparently that's a long shot. You cannot say a girl you love her after you had sex, that means apparently you want more sex and since you're creep and do not know how to talk to women too much you simply say the most outrageous thing which turns them off and resulting in kicking of your ass out and conclusion: – you got nothing, neither the sex nor the girl.

So making me realise that I should keep things slow before it picks up, I took the liberty of going back to my apartment in the hope of writing and apparently I got a good story plot by our conversation.

Life gives you simple things to play with and sometimes we people make it complicating instead of finishing the game simpler.

9. Having a Friend

I thought about giving a call to Chutiya but since he hasn't called since our last encounter on an early Saturday morning, I thought it would be rather great to leave him alone as he has some stuff to deal with and apparently Darshana is a big deal for him. They met at a party a few years back and started dating and since then they're still stuck at that. I on the other hand, met Mona through mutual friends, had sex, started dating, more sex, moving in, she got pregnant and therefore eventually marriage. I wasn't exactly sure about it but since ours is a more conservative society, we had to marry. But we weren't happy and the sex was dull so we divorced. Long story short, if I would have put the condom in every time we had sex, we still would have been dating. But that's history and now I am a self-depressed bastard son-of-a-bitch who doesn't care anything apart from his children, well apparently correcting that sentence since I couldn't care more about Rima. Well doing nothing in the apartment is my common hobby and as usual too tired to even comment upon a basic requirement like getting up from the couch to drink some water but I am lazy as hell, don't like to spend energy on stupid if it isn't really important.

Opening my laptop, I thought about a possible turnover to the story, like a twist. Opened MS-Word but my fingers stopped typing and mind stopped imagining. It's like my body suddenly stopped at the thought of writing. I am not that good at writing love stories, I mean I'm useless in the area but since today's youth loved reading about stupid shit that aint true stuff so be it. It's like an Indian soap opera with a definite ending at precise 250 pages average.

Distraction is the thing which causes every other person to lose his ability to work. It usually happens when you get an erection and having an erection in the most awkward situation is another factor to deal with. I mean seriously if you're talking to a friend who is going through a bad breakup and suddenly your dick is up just because you thought that your friend's girlfriend is hot and out of nowhere you start to fantasize about yourself with her and go as much as far to plan a future together but that's just up to the level of banging her. Once that's done you look for the next hunt and that's what's going on in today's generation. Yeah there are some lovebirds who want to take the next step but due to society pressure they break it off. But No I am not going from distraction to nationalism. I am just a flamboyant writer who got a Pulitzer 5 years ago just because he wrote a story about a begging boy and his life and hardships and apparently the jury loved the simple thing so much that they gave me that award which put me to pressure to write another award selling by my publisher which in turn made me arrogant which led to my drinking and in fact made my way to jail to some harassment and concluding with two divorces and 3 children. Sometimes I really miss being the good old Pulitzer prize winning writer but now as the fame has gone and I'm close to poverty, I sometimes feel like I never should have been a writer.

I was a good old fashioned PR in a respectable MNC but due to my rebellious nature and casual approach towards life and as because I am passionate about what I am, I quit the job, started writing and now where am I, in an old cubicle down Old Bandra. Living the dream. Seriously being passionate is not as easy as it sounds. It takes a lot of failures to reach where I was and lot of stupid decisions to where I am.

Read the whole manuscript twice but like something was missing. But couldn't guessed what.

Never realised when I was fast asleep and the by the time I woke up, it was 630 in the evening and I haven't had lunch yet. I wasn't feeling hungry but a good fruit might help my stomach I thought. Went over to the fridge to take out apples which had been there for the past 2 weeks. It was a gift from the old neighbour living downstairs. Well gotta thank her for that. A violent knock on the door startled me and went over to answer the door. It was Chutiya and he was looking worse. As if he got hit by a truck. Whoa, looking at this fucking bastard this damn serious was something like looking at an asshole turning into a corpse without a coffin. But man I was getting a little worried.

I pushed him to sit at the couch. He obliged at first but took it eventually. I brought him a glass of water and waited for him to talk.

He drank the water and was asking for weed. Instead, I brought him a cigarette.

"What happened?" I said lighting his cigarette

Puffing smoke out of his nose, he went for the traditional 2 minute silence to deepen the situation but as I was impatient and reckless, I gave a soft slap on his face and made him talk by shaking him.

"We broke up" He said after some hesitation

"What? Again?" I said

He looked me in the eye with utmost hate "Yes you motherfucker AGAIN!!!"

That was harsh from his sad but I let it go because he was upset and I was insensitive.

"Sorry man, you need some drinks?" I asked

"Hell yeah, bring me whiskey"

"I don't have any, I just got beers" I said

He suddenly stood up "Lets go" he said and started dragging me

"Wait where?" I asked

"To bang girls"

"What the hell are you talking about? You just broke up, you seriously want to take the opportunity here?"

"Why not? She thinks I'm cheating on her" he said and started crying

Man, my son crying is a thing and this fucker crying is another, I mean dealing with kids is easy compared to being with a grown up man. I tried to console him and gave him more water to drink.

"You ok man?" I asked after listening to his wailing for 2 minutes

"Why man, why, why the fuck can't she understand the fuck that I love her and I need her for the rest of my life"

"Maybe you did something wrong back in the day"

He suddenly looked at me with his teary eyes.

"What the fuck do you mean? I cheated on her, is that what you saying?" he suddenly turned angry at my comment.

"Nah man, that's not what I meant" I defended myself

"Then what the fuck do you mean?"

"I mean maybe you said something wrong while trying to explain yourself to her" Wow, didn't know where did that came from

"I said something wrong?" he said with a much calmer voice. Good, he bought it.

"Yeah, girls are very sensitive to every word her guy says to her and something may hurt her that much that she takes the final step in the relationship."

"But she doesn't have the right to take that" he said

"Apparently she did just that so…" I said, handing him a beer from the fridge.

Sigh

"You got some weed?" he asked

"Nah, we finished the last pack weeks ago"

He suddenly brought out the pack from his pocket

"Where did you get these?" I asked, happy that I will get high

"I always have a emergency stashed with myself" he said with pride

"Really, knock it off" I knew he was lying

He was smiling. Gotcha kid

"I took some off killing"

"Ha-ha, I knew you need to get high"

"Apparently I knew that too" he said. Killing was our dealer and usually brought us every weed possibly made.

He made the rolls and lighted them up. After a few joints, we were on cloud nine.

"Fuck her man, she didn't even gave me a blowjob" he said

"I thought you banged her" I said, totally out of mind what the fuck I was saying

"Banging is not as equal to giving head, I wanted her so much to give me a head but the bitch always told me jerk off as if she knows I'm hungry for sex"

"Fuck her man, I just want to be high" I said, carefully putting down the words together in my mouth to utter

"Yeah, fuck her" he said after 30 second breakdown

We were totally high, I took my 5th joint. Chutiya passed out eventually. I took a look at my laptop as it was on sleep mode and tilted my head towards the clock to check the time. It was 9.

I had nothing to go on that time so puffing out the smoke, I passed out.

10. The Main Element

It was Tuesday, the day when usually people tend to eat vegetarian. It wasn't exactly a rule made by the government but it was a social rule made for people to give up chicken for one fucking day. I usually don't believe in restrictions but I do believe in higher power. But the fact that you have to eat vegan or take a fast just to impress the almighty isn't really my call. So rather that, I usually take a nice city trip checking out few restaurants, especially the ones those are new.

I wake up and find myself in the dinner table, not recalling what the fuck happened. I wake up, clearing my eye dirt out and seeing Karan checking out my laptop.

"When did you wake up?" I asked

He turned to look towards me

"10 minutes ago"

I went up and washed my face. Took a towel to dry it and he was still staring at my lappy.

"What are you looking at?" I said as I went over to check it too

He was looking at my work upto where I was heading. Till now, I could only manage to write 8 pages and I had a minimum limit of 100. The story as far goes from the good old poor boy, falls in love with a rich girl and apparently it's going to turn into DDLJ if I don't come with a creativity.

"It's missing something" he said, still staring at the screen

"Yeah, but I don't know what"

"SEX" he said

"What?"

"The main element for a novel"

"Are you fucking kidding me?" I went over to my bedroom to get my car keys.

"Yeah man, you totally need some spice to mix it up" he said as he came following me to the bedroom

He had a point. I mean I took the liberal of writing this shit just because it has a sex angle to it but if I don't put it, people may not look it. Even though how much we say we are developed, we are still developing and apparently writing sex plays a key role in it.

"How?" I said softly, picking up the car keys

"You don't know how to write about sex?" he said with a big LOL in his face

Damn, I was embarrassed but he was so fucking right. It's not easy to write intimate moments, I mean not everyone has the ability to just fantasize about it and type. I'm 41 for Christ's sake.

"Ha ha, man okay I'm going to teach you then" he said

He was suddenly in high moods after he got the idea and apparently forgot that he broke up yesterday with his 5 year long girlfriend but that didn't mattered to him rather than he took the responsibility of making me write about sex.

"Okay, first things first, for writing about sex, you need to embrace it" he said after I locked my apartment

"What the fuck do you mean by 'embrace'?"

"That means you need to have lots of sex"

"And what made you think that I would agree to that" I said with a strong sarcasm in my voice

"Man, I know you'd strongly oppose to this but think about it, man, pleasure plus money, eh?" he was hoping for a positive response

"Fuck you I mean not going to have sex"

"What then? You are gonna jerk off, well good luck with that" he said, Sarcasm

"Okay, lets assume I approve this, how am I going to have sex. Sex is two way traffic. You know that I need a woman for it, right?" I said with utmost polite for this asshole. Just because I can't write about sex doesn't conclude that I should have sex.

"Don't worry, I have a number…" he said

"I am not going to have sex with prostitutes" I snapped

He nodded. Apparently thinking that his mission might be on the verge for destruction.

"If I am going to have sex, the woman must agree to it too" I said and at the same time felt proud.

"Oh shut the fuck up. Don't give me that crap speech about women empowerment, you're not Rahul Gandhi"

Okay he was right, I wasn't

"Yeah but you got the point what I am trying to say right?" I asked

"Yeah fucker I got it"

We got to my car placed in the basement. I started the ignition of my Maruti Suzuki ZEN bought about 7 years from now. It's still a cool car.

"So what's the game plan?" he asked

"What? What game plan?"

"How the fuck you are going to bang?"

"That's out of the equation okay, think of plan B"

"I don't have any"

"Yeah, I know you don't cause you're an asshole"

"Hmmm"

We reached the local joint, a new place for usually college-goers but we were too matured to enter there. But since I need something in the stomach so I didn't gave a head about where I am. Still, it was awkward

We ordered for sandwiches. Chutiya was looking in my right.

"Check out that chick man, 9'0 clock" he said

I turned towards right and saw some girls staring at us and smiling and laughing among themselves. We had no option but to smile back.

"Man, If I have been 5 years younger, I would have nailed her" he said

"Yeah right"

"I am serious man, Look, just check her boobs man shit"

"Shut up man, this is a public place" I said, trying to concentrate on the sandwich which was just brought to us

"Yeah as if the government is going to arrest us, eh?" he said out loud. Some heads turned towards us

"Shut up" trying to be as discrete as possible

Chutiya was somehow disturbed because yeah he is an asshole but he would never go on to say 'Bang random chicks'. Apparently something was bothering him and he desperately wanted sex and he wanted me as a wingman for his score. Darshana really broke him. Fucking bitch.

"Dude, let's just eat the sandwich and leave, I'm paying so don't worry" I said

"You know" he said

"What?"

"I just can't stop thinking about her"

Man, he is so screwed. I faced like him when I was dating Radhika but apparently that turned into a mistake.

"Listen, you need to calm down" I said

"Sid?" said a female voice from behind

We both got surprised and turned 12'0 clock. It was the girl I banged Thursday night, Zerifa, now I remember after like three meetings. What a dick I am

"Hey, Zerifa, right?" trying to be as subtle as possible. She brought in a few girlfriends of her. Chutiya raised his eyebrows and I was trying not to embarrass myself.

"Yeah, you remember my name this time" she giggled along with her friends.

"Is this the writer guy you're talking about, Z? Kind of hot isn't he?" said one of the girls in the group and all of them broke into laughter.

Chutiya was starting to smile and giving me 'What the fuck' look.

"I didn't know you come here" she giggled again

"No. I mean this is my first time" I said with great difficulty

"Really, hope you're finding it cool here" she said by looking me in the eye.

"Yeah, yeah it's it's cool here"

"Have to tell you, you're not going to find shots here" she said and everyone including chutiya broke into laughter. Why the fuck is he laughing about

"Yeah, listen I have to go" signalling chutiya to move

We came out of the joint and went towards the car.

Sitting inside, "What the fuck just happened?" said he

"I don't know"

"How the fuck does she know you?"

I looked towards him and gave him the 'you know' look

"You banged her"

Shit

"You fucking banged her, shit, when?"

Suddenly, someone was knocking on the window screen of the car. It was Zerifa

I turned down the screen, "Can we talk?" she said

"Yeah but I got this gig...." I said and looked towards chutiya who was eagerly trying to eavesdrop

"Just for a minute, please" she asked politely. No point to argue I guess so I got off from the car.

"Sorry, please forgive me" she said. Yeah right

"You just embarrassed me in front of hundred people, it's not easy to get an apology" I said, anger in my voice

"Well apparently, I wanted to teach you a lesson this time"

"What?" I said, shocked at her explanation

"Yeah, but you remember my name so I thought maybe I have some importance after all in your life" she explained

"You got that just by hearing your name uttered by me? Wow, okay" Cool explanation, still irrational.

"I also made my friends made fun of you so I'm sorry for that too" she said

Wow, getting a girl's apology is epic but still it was genuine so I thought maybe I should forgive her

"Let me make it up to you" she said

"How?" seriously how?

"Can we go out to dinner tomorrow?" she said

"Are you asking me out?" I said, delighted

"Yeah, don't make it obvious, pick me up at 7 from my apartment?" she said

Wow, a girl asking out. Two on two. Girl apologising and asking you out is like a dream come true and apparently everything happens but in reverse.

"Yeah sure, I will call you"

"Yeah right" she snapped

My eyebrows suddenly rose

"Sorry, it's just that you promised to call but you never did and now apparently I am giving you a second chance" she said

"I am not going to waste it, I promise" I said. Hellbind I guess

She was satisfied by my answer and asked her if I could drop her off but she politely declined and so I went over to my car to start it off and zoomed away.

"Who the fuck was she? How many times you banged her?" Chutiya asked. Getting curious by every question

"None of your business" I snapped quickly

"Okay" he smiled "Still I respect you" he continued

"For what?" I looked at him

"That you still got it"

"Got what?"

"You know the charm, that is needed to bed girls"

"What the fuck, man. Are you an asshole?"

"You always call me by that name"

"Yeah but I don't expect you to be one"

"Sorry"

There was silence, complete silence till we reached Malad.

"How was the sex?" he suddenly asked

Our eyes suddenly brightened and we started giggling

"It was epic"

"Yeah, she gave you a blowjob?"

"Yup, I love when a woman does that" I said, recalling those moments

"Every man does"

We started laughing and screamed slangs for the people to notice. It was really an insane act to do but still when you got friends, you always need to do something insane because memories born from those moments.

"How were her boobs?"

"Shut the fuck up"

"Whoa, sorry"

Again silence. Men really don't take really too much time to make the situation complicated. Still they're better off than women who usually prefer to hide behind those hypocrite faces instead of showing their true colours.

"Can you ask you something?" he suddenly said

"Hope it's not part of her body"

"No but what was she saying out of the car?"

"She asked me out"

"Whoa, really?"

"Yeah"

"Wow man, it usually happens the opposite"

Suddenly I felt proud that a girl asked me out, that too a guy close to double her age. Girls should know, even if boy takes the initiative of asking her out, they should do it too because once in a while every guy deserves a chance.

"What if it's a pity?" he suddenly asked, breaking my thought

"What do you mean?"

"Like charity"

"Charity?"

"Yeah, like I am doing a favour for the old man"

"What?" I said

"Yeah man, girls browse old men just for the sex because they also know how good and experienced they are compared to the youth of our country."

"That's not fucking true" I said, a little doubt in my voice

"Okay just let me get this straight. A girl comes over, checks you out and takes you to her place and has sex and finally wants to go out on a date with you even though she clearly knows there's no fucking future in this and eventually it will end."

"Shut up okay, just shut the fuck up before I hit you" I said, blood pressure suddenly rising up and realising that chutiya was talking sense. Was she doing me a favour? I don't want favours. I can have sex with whoever I want and date whoever I want. Can't I? But I'm old and I have kids, alimony, pay checks and bills and I can't support even if I get into a relationship and who knows even if there's a future or not.

"You may be right" I said, looking straight on the road after like 2 minutes of silence

Sigh "I am sorry man" he said

"Nah but I have to ask her before I end it"

"Nah man, that's a bad idea"

"No, if she is doing me a favour, I need to know and I have a call on this, not you" I said, deciding that there's a whole lot to it.

I turned the cab towards home because at that moment I remembered Suresh wanted me more than what I wanted myself for more.

11. Twist and Turns

"Suresh wanted to move on from the rejection he got from his first and only love, Naina. So he took up drinking and gambling and made his life HELL!!!!!"

"Yeah what the fuck happened to love and sex shit" I said, referring to what chutiya was saying

"Yeah the love is still the topic but we still need a twist, right?"

"And for that you assumed the girl's rejection" I said, bored

"Yeah why? you're thinking like some type of DDLJ remake"

"Apparently yeah"

"You asshole fuck"

"What?" I said looking at the laptop screen

"India has come a long way since that. DDLJ times are over and only murder times are flourishing"

"Yeah because of assholes like you, nobody gives a damn anymore to love"

We went back to the story. Seriously why the fuck was I writing this shit, I mean literally what sin did I commit that I came to the level of writing shitty love stories just for paying my bills and alimony.

"You should have read more love stories instead of historical ones"

"Yeah I know"

Apparently I should have but romanticism isn't my thing. Maybe that's why I ended up having two divorces.

It was already 11 on the clock of Wednesday morning and I had to go the market to buy things for the next week. I got ready and took the list and went out. Didn't wanted chutiya to come because I love shopping by my myself.

It took me an hour to reach the nearest supermarket because of traffic jams of Mumbai. I hate it when I get late.

It took me another hour to do shopping because I wasn't that good in shopping and I usually preferred branded and healthy. So browsing takes me a lot of time.

"You rather need Amul instead of Mother Diary" said someone from behind while I was checking out milk section.

I turned to look and it was Radhika. She was wearing a yellow salwaar kameez that had a fine half sleeve and a gold tip on her forehead suited her attire. She was looking amazingly beautiful.

"Hey Hi" I said, completely surprised to see her

We hugged and I kind of checked her out. She was looking so fucking hot and even I can see her nipular area through her salwaar. I guess she wore a transparent bra.

"So you shopping?" she said

It was fairly obvious but as courtesy "Yeah, it's umm you know my weekly shopping" I said, trying not to look at her boobs

She is so beautiful even when she's going to reach 40s within a few years but still she maintained herself.

We checked out together after paying our respective bills.

"So how did you come?" I asked, just to make small talk

"I took a bus" she said and indirectly asking me to drop her home. Women are really fucking good with manipulation and seduction because they know they're beautiful and somehow or the other they tend to take advantage of their beauty.

"C'mon I will drop you home" as this was the most obvious thing to do

She resisted at first but I knew she was delighted by the offer so eventually she agreed. Women will first resist but eventually will come around and this thing most of the boys out there don't know and fall prey to rejection phobia.

She sat on my bike with her hands on my shoulder. Kind of felt glad that she did.

It took us like 90 minutes to reach her place and we were totally silent during that moment. I thought maybe she doesn't want me to talk to her and so let it be.

She went over to open the door and I took all her carry bags to the house. I put them on the kitchen floor as she went to the bedroom.

As I was heading out, she suddenly yelled "We need to talk"

Sigh, I went over to sit on the couch. Rima wasn't home as she was probably on school. I really miss those golden days when we were all together, happy and most importantly we had each other's backs. But I guess situation changes with times.

She changed herself into a maxi and went over to the kitchen to get me some water. I took the glass from her hand as she sat down across from me. I drank the water and put the glass back on the table.

She was rubbing her hands, probably preparing herself to talk about something that has been running through her mind for quite some time now. I just wanted to get out of there as soon as possible because I had fucking work to do but when a women says she wants to talk, apparently she wants you to listen to what she has to say.

"I umm broke up with Suraj" she said as she was looking for words to say and apparently she broke down.

When a women breaks down she wants you to console her. Apparently most of the guys can do that perfectly and end up being friendzoned or brozoned. I wasn't there to fucking waste my time all the way from my place to hers just to fucking console her as I had work to do.

"I am sorry to hear that" I said with total coldness

"He was so perfect for me as if we were meant for each other" she was wiping her tears and crying more.

I stood up; I couldn't take this crap about how perfect her boyfriend was in front of me.

"What happened? Sit down" she said

"I can't" I said, not looking at her

"What you can't?" she said, also standing up

"I can't listen to your wailing just because you got dumped"

"I didn't said that I got dumped" she said, getting serious by every word

"Oh yeah, you're crying, you said to me last time that he was younger than you. Do I need to make it more obvious?"

She felt silent "I need to be alone" she suddenly said

I got it, she felt bad because I had drawn her obvious but I didn't wanted things bad between us as like between Mona and me.

"I am sorry, I really am, please forgive me" I said, trying to apologise

She nodded. Probably not interested in it.

"Before I go I just wanted to say that you're the best thing that ever happened to me and because that dick left you, it was his fault and you deserve better, because still for me you're one of the most gorgeous women I have ever seen" I said, looking into her eyes.

She was looking in to my eyes with her eyes being wet. I was looking in to her lips at that very moment and suddenly out of nowhere, I kissed her. I kissed her like after 5 years and we were exploring each other's mouth by our tongues and couldn't stop kissing each other for like at least 2 minutes after which we pulled ourselves out as we needed air to breathe.

I started pressing her boobs and opened her top two buttons of her maxi, she was pulling my dick through my pants. I opened my pants as she was coming out of her maxi. She was naked and beautiful and the last time that I saw her naked body was like 5–6 years back. We felt intimate that moment as we were laughing together. She started giving me a head. It was fucking good. She was still my best blowjob ever. I took her to the bedroom and we were on the missionary position because we always made love like that. Even Rima was born because of this position. No matter what, this made us bring closer to each other. She started screaming and I started pushing my penis hard into her vagina. She was screaming hard as I was making her wet. We came together and it felt so fucking good. The last time I had sex with her was at a charity function when my book was a big success and we were special guests for the occasion. Those were the good old days but still coming inside a women's vagina is far better than jerking off and people should have sex more than masturbate. It's kind of like my personal opinion.

I passed out after cuming and woke up after I got hungry. It was already 3 in the afternoon. She was sleeping peacefully beside me and I could have been looking at her face forever. I got up and went over to the fridge to eat an apple. An apple a day keeps the doctor away but for me it keeps my hunger away. Fine by that.

I checked my phone and chutiya already called me 3 times and whatsapped me on where I was.

I went back to bed and she suddenly woke up.

"You okay?" she asked

Looking at her naked, how could anyone felt being not okay. I smiled at her and she smiled back.

"You're so beautiful" I said, pushing back her hair from her face

She smiled as well as blushed. We were cuddling

"You know?" she said

"What?"

"I was thinking"

"About?"

"Well you know"

No I don't, come to the point woman

"What?"

"We were so good together"

"Yeah we were"

"And I still think of the times that we became one"

One as in she was referring to the times we fucked each other. Apparently girls called it 'being one' and guys called it 'banging or fucking'.

"Yeah"

"Do you?" she asked, looking in my eyes

"I do. I still think of the times we were together as a family"

"Hmmm"

Okay I don't know what angle she was playing but I could make it out that she is trying to be nostalgic and I hate sharing my nostalgic memories.

"You know, we can be" she said

"What?" shit, she was going to ask me if we can get back together. SHIT

"We can be together again" she said and started looking in my eyes, seeing in her eyes was hope but I can't but I cannot tell her directly. I have to be subtle as possible.

"Umm, you know ah "

"Yes?" she was being very polite and patient. I could sense that in her voice

"I didn't know that you were thinking about that"

"Yeah and I think we still have each other"

"What made you realise that?"

"You know Suraj is something like you and I realised that I always wanted you and maybe we can work things out and you can still have that family you always missed"

Wow, is she fucking kidding with me because if she isn't, she played a long shot down the park and this thing for me is next to impossible. I mean When our marriage ended, my love for her was destroyed and it took me a lot of time to move on and she suddenly expects me to be her rebound.

"I can't" I said, I was trying to be as honest as possible.

She was disappointed "Why? I thought you said you missed us being together"

"Yeah I said but that's a long time ago and I don't want to be in a relationship anymore. I am good being single" I said with a little bit of lies

She sat up, her boobs were flouting "Then why the hell did you fuck me?" Okay she was angry and sad and I totally get that because becoming one turning into fuck in a momentary time really brings out the disappointment in a person.

"I made love to you because deep down I still love you and yeah I wanted to be as close to you as possible" I said, trying to bring some fucked up love back

She became silent; I guess she bought it, phew

She got up from the bed and started wearing her clothes. It is amazing how women look beautiful when they change.

"I have to go the temple" she said and went to the dressing table.

I guess she was trying to tell me to go. Apparently I know some of women's indirect way to say something after seeing two of them dumping me and out of them, one tried to reconcile which I turned down because deep down I also knew it was not going to work. So why take the chance and end up paying

I went out of her house and kick-started the bike. Chutiya was calling me several times. I reached my place within an hour and saw chutiya waiting for me near the entrance of my apartment building.

"Where the fuck were you?" He asked

"Went for a long drive"

"And where are the shopping's that you went out in the morning to buy"

Shit, left them at Radhika's house and now I can't even get them back.

"I uh forgot them at the store"

"You fuck, what the hell were you doing? Checking out someone's ass" he said and broke into laughter

"Why are outside and is my door locked?"

"Yeah, your door's locked and apparently I made some changes to the story"

"Like?"

"Like the boy will be going through a life and death situation"

"That's bullshit"

"Yeah but still today's people love it so I am adding it up"

"Is this your book or mine?"

"It's yours but as your agent, I have a duty to help you in your crisis"

"Yeah, yeah" I said and lighted a cigarette

Cigarettes are good sometimes. Passes your time and makes you feel high, but not like marijuana. It's another stuff but still all these are bad and should never be practised or else people will get censored.

"I still couldn't figure it out why the fuck is the 'Tobacco Kills' is on the cigarette cover. It's so fucking useless" I said, puffing out smoke

We both broke into laughter.

12. The Date

It was already 630 and I got only half an hour to pick up my date. I was in my best suit with a blue shirt tucked with a nice stripped tie. I usually wore this suit on special occasions and as today was one of them. Apparently because it was a long time since I last time went out on a date. But practically or not, I am too old now for such tactics but since a girl asked me out and that too I have a probability of having sex with her again or rather I put it to see her beautiful naked body, well putting down my reasons aside, I take my handkerchief and sprayed my chanel perfume. I took the car keys as I washed it today for this special occasion with great care and was feeling happy from inside. I mean everyday feels great when they go out on a date and ours is so conservative country and doesn't give values to western methods for mating, it really makes an impact on one's lives when they get to know that they're going out on a date. There's the eye-contact rule, the hand touch rule, the simultaneous eyes and lips look where you make the other person think that you want to kiss them. There's that leg touch rule and some of them even go further ahead of taking the leg further into the junk. There are numerous rules and one of the most famous is the 3 date rule where you have to have sex with your date, like it or not and it is one of the best rules implemented in modern times.

So fantasizing about my date and lifting my moods, I walk to my car, start it and take off. It took me 20 minutes to reach there as I had already putted 80 on my mileage clock, thank god no cops saw me.

I went up to her door and knocked. She took precisely 2 minutes to answer as she was putting make-up on her face. I could say she was looking stunning and apparently the most beautiful women I have ever seen.

"Just wait for 5 minutes" she said and directed me to seat on the couch.

The 5 minute rule of women is the most dangerous rule, they apparently say 5 minutes but it takes them like 20 to 30 minutes to get ready. Apparently most of the guys out there mind this rule and hate it but for me it's cool, I mean if a women is getting ready just to look amazing for me, I have no problem with that.

She took 15 minutes (Less than what I had expected) to come out of her bedroom, the bedroom where we had the most amazing sex. People say that never date your ONS because it makes things awkward but for me it's all new so quick judging might not be appropriate.

We went to a simple restaurant down near the Gateway of India. We took a centre table and ordered for water. She took the menu and started browsing for the dinner. I had a question, who's going to pay? Because if we keep things straight, she asked me out and she should be paying but it doesn't take long for the tables to turn.

"Don't worry I am paying" she said giggling and biting her lower lip. She was looking gorgeous.

Wow, that really put down the burden. Seriously girls, you should pay sometimes too because why should you always be dependent on men to pay for your bills. I can say that this girl is independent and the most wonderful girl I have ever seen in recent times.

We ordered for one fried rice with paneer butter masala along with a chicken tikka. Seemed reasonable for dinner.

"So?" she asked, putting down the menu and apparently crossing her arms and looking at me

"So?" I said, trying to figure out the best possible answer to her every question

"How's things?" she said smiling. I thought she was referring to the sex we had, but I know women don't like to talk about sex in a date

"Things are okay, I guess" I said with showing her my most honest face

"Tell me" She said

"Tell you what?"

"What happened to you since we last met"

She was just asking me because I know how curious she was. What should I tell her, Rima, Book or the fact that I had sex this afternoon with Radhika.

"Nothing much"

"C'mon tell me" she said and touched my hand. It kind of gave me Goosebumps.

"Nothing really" I don't want to tell her how fucked up I was

"Okay" she said, I could sense her disappointment in her voice.

"What?" trying to cool off the escalating tension

"I told you before" she said, angrily

"Told me what?"

"That it's not going to work if you're not honest" she said, apparently standing up to leave

"No, no please wait, I am sorry, please forgive me, please sit down" I said, trying desperately to calm her down.

She closed her eyes and calmed herself down. She sat down and took a deep breath.

"I am sorry, it's just that I have some trust issues" I said, trying to sound as genuine as possible

"Seriously?? You have trust issues with the person you had sex with" she said, frustrated by my explanation

"I am sorry, it's just that the manuscript, the children and the ex-wives are putting a lot of problem on my hand

She was silent. Guess she was interested. W, I mean it really mans a lot when somebody is interested in listening to your problem.

"You can talk. It always helps" she said with her eyes lit

"Yeah but I am not really an open person. I usually prefer keeping to myself"

"Yeah I know how it feels if someone betrays your trust" she said and it was like she was recalling her past

There was total silence between us. Apparently the food was the ice breaker.

We ate and talked about stuffs like passion, art and music. I asked her what made her to come to journalism to which she replied that journalism was her calling.

"How come you started writing?" she asked and was looking into my eyes.

She was something way too personal but I guess it doesn't mind to share the experience on how something from a hobby turned into your profession.

"You know it all started when I realised that I can write good stories for the school magazine and apparently someone told me to give a shot at these and one thing led to another and now I am a writer" I said smiling, I always loved to talk about how I became a writer

"Well I am happy that you followed your dreams" she said and she was touching my thigh with her leg

Dreams? I wouldn't say that I mean it was just a hobby which kind of was a one long shot which made into reality due to readers only. Everything what I am is because of readers or the ones who buys my books. I always get the revenue which helps in paying my bills. The way that her leg was going upwards, I guessed she wanted sex badly. But girls are confusing so Can't really make the conclusion

"Why you are also doing that?" I said, trying to refer both the terms

She giggled "What do you mean?"

"Both"

She laughed as we ate, the food was awesome. Especially the Paneer really matched the fried rice. One of the best combined dishes I ever had

"Yeah I always decide whatever I want" she said as she was going up and started rubbing my dick with her left leg.

It was turning me on. I mean what the hell is this girl up to?

"I think we shouldn't" I said, trying to be as subtle as possible.

"Why?" she was going ahead with her plan

My dick was up and apparently was ready to take off. The waiter came for the bill. I paid him quickly and she laughed seeing my desperation. We quickly went to her place and as she unlocked the door, we started kissing. She was unlocking my belt and opened my zip whereas I was pressing her perfect tits.

We moved to her bedroom and we were undressing ourselves. Suddenly one think struck me, the thought that chutiya told me yesterday about young girls. Why the fuck was she having sex with me? Just because I am far more experienced guy and she needed training before she can get to the real arena. The thought about how come a father of three, two divorces and apparently an asshole who was going to be broke within the next week is getting laid with a beautiful college girl. It's very unlikely to be so fucking true. Why the fuck would she see me as a future? And apparently how the hell is our society going to accept that a man double her age is banging a girl so hot. Many questions were popping in my head and suddenly I lost my erection. She was giving me a blowjob by that time and suddenly saw my dick getting shrieked up.

"What happened?" she said as she looked up seeing my face

I was rather confused on what the hell I should do? Should I go?

"What happened to him?" she said, stretching my dick like a balloon with no air

"I have to go" I said and reached for my pants

"Why? What happened?" she said, confused

"I have a client early next morning and I desperately need some sleep" I said, reasonable for her I guess

"Why didn't you tell me?" she asked, crestfallen she was

"It was a last minute deal and I didn't expected to make love tonight" Using the word love helps in case you're with a girl.

She sighed and yawned. I quickly dressed and got out of there as soon as possible. On my way back, I was thinking this may not be good, It's surely not good, no not fucking good. I am not a good guy in relationships and neither is chutiya but still he has got Darshana and I am not going to let it end as they are both made for each other. So I took a long turn back and took the road to the suburbs.

I knocked on the door of 12/E. I wanted to talk sense into Darshana and I knew she is a smart girl and will take back Karan. I know these two are made for each other. It took Darshana like 10 minutes to answer.

"What are you doing here?" she said, probably confused

"Listen I think we need to talk" I said, trying to sound as serious as possible

"Can't we do this later?" she said, trying to hide behind the door

"No, we need to talk. I may not find a better time" I said, I was finding her rather more suspicious

"Listen, I will give you a call okay?" she said, she was trying desperately to not let me in her house.

"Why? I need to talk and it's pretty fucking serious"

"Listen it's already 11 and I think you shouldn't be here and it will take a long time for you to reach your apartment Sid. Please you need to go" she said

"Fine, just get me some water and I'll go" I said

"Wait" she said and went to her kitchen to get some

I asked her for water just to distract her to let me inside. I went in and saw male clothes here and there. I went to her bedroom to peep and saw a guy was smoking cigarette and checking his cell. She saw me peeping her bedroom and was apparently embarrassed.

"You bitch" I couldn't say anymore and walked out.

I didn't stop until I started my car and went off. I can't believe that she moved on. I mean chutiya here was crying for her and was possibly thinking of a way to get back together and she was having sex with other men. I was so sad for chutiya, I mean the guy was living a lie with that bitch. I mean seriously girls why the fuck do you do that and especially when a guy truly loves you and wants to be with you for the rest of his life and that's a big step for a man who usually runs off from commitment issues just to stay bachelor and when the moment they realise they found the women they get heartbroken and eventually take revenge on the whole female population by having ONS.

I was fucked up and apparently all I did was trying to save a relationship which never existed. I went back to blueberry and ordered Prateek to bring large sized shots and told him to keep them coming. I drank my heart out and the next moment I know, I was sleeping on the couch of my apartment and chutiya was typing for me in the laptop.

I woke up and tried some lemon just to get over the hangover.

"What the fuck are you writing about?" checking my laptop and seeing Suresh Yadav with a new lease in life

"I thought that maybe he was missing a business opportunity so I gave him one" he said, he was looking satisfied

"Apparently so" I said, I couldn't remember anything from last night since I left sex with Zerifa.

"Yeah and maybe he can be a better person than just falling in love"

"I thought this book was about love"

"It is but with a twist"

Sigh

I checked the time and it was 11 in the morning.

"What day is it?" I asked, confused what was yesterday

"It's Thursday"

13. Out of the Blue

Fuck, I got one week more to complete the shit and I haven't even reached 20 pages. It's going to fucking kill me

"Where were you last night?" he asked suddenly, still looking at the laptop

"What do you mean?"

"I mean, if you had sex then Prateek would never brought you over unless you are gay and drunk"

"Shut the fuck up"

"I am just asking. Where the fuck were you?" he said, looking at me

"I cannot even recall that where the fuck I was after the dinner"

"Oh, how was the dinner?"

"It was good"

"Yeah"

"And?"

"And what?"

"Did she invite you over?"

"For?" I said, probably knew what the fuck he was going to ask but I needed to remember last night

"Sex, you dumbass"

"Yeah she did"

"And?"

"We. Had. Sex" trying to jitter the words together

"How was it?"

How can I fake it "It was awesome"

"Yeah?"

"Yeah, I mean it"

"Like the last time?"

"Better"

"Really?"

"Yeah, what do you want? A certificate" getting irritated

"No, just saying" he said, still looking at me

I went over to the fridge to look for food but I probably forgot that I left it yesterday at Radhika's house after having sex. Shit, I was starving.

"Do we have something to eat?"

"Apart from water, I don't think so"

"How the fuck did you had dinner then?"

"I ordered Pizza"

"Well I think we have to do it again"

"Okay but these time you're paying"

"Oh yeah, who the fuck is staying in whose house? You should pay up the food expenses, asshole"

"Okay, fair point well made"

I went over to drink some water just to kill off the starvation while chutiya was making the call to dominoes.

I tried to recall what the fuck happened from last night but apparently so I couldn't and everything was in blur. Maybe I shouldn't have drank too much but why the fuck did I took those shots? Just because I was angry, just because I couldn't let my dick get the better of my morality. No, certainly not. There must be something else which just became blank and if Prateek dropped me then certainly I went over to the bar to drink and since I can't recall, I must have drank hard. I usually drink hard when I am fucking angry or sad or just need to kill some time.

"I called the dominoes and ordered chicken with extra chesses on top" he said

"Yeah, you better have the money cause I don't"

"We will split it"

"I don't have money to even split"

"Guess you're broke right now"

"Totally"

"What about the book then?"

"Apparently I got one week more and if I don't bring a story by then with an ending, my ass will get fired"

"Don't worry man, we can do it" he said, patting my shoulders

"Yeah dumbass, you're investment will not be doubled just because you still think I can do it"

"Hmmm, let's see though"

"Yeah, fuck my ass if you want to see it" I said, I don't why but I felt frustrated and irritated

"Hey, what's with the attitude?" he asked, probably because I never replied him back so harsh

"Nothing"

He came up to me and I can assume he was getting angry

"Just because I am helping you to write your story doesn't mean that I have your back. I am just using a metaphor and I fucking want you to write it. Write the goddamn book" he screamed at the last sentence

Whoa, never expected him to lose himself

"You alright man?" I asked, concerned

"Do I fucking look like I am alright?"

"I just want to look out for you man"

"Yeah? How?" he suddenly was looking me in the eye and I pretty much assumed that he was using sarcasm on me. How the fuck did this morning turned into a complicated shit.

"I don't know like calling you from time to time just to check on you"

"Yeah, you did that for checking on me?"

"Yeah...."

"No you motherfucking son of a bitch. You didn't do that to check on me, you did that because you didn't wanted to get alone"

Whoa, he was crossing the line here

"Oh, so you think I am a loner?"

"Loner? Loner would be improvement. I think you're one fucked isolated asshole who has nothing, nothing whatsoever and will die soon, not because he smokes or drinks. But because he will feel the void inside of him which will make him realise that he is dead for the world and nobody fucking wants him"

That's it, I punched him in the face and he grabbed my neck and I was kicking his foot while he kept on punching me on my belly. We fell down and he was choking me and I tried to scratch his face but he got the advantage and was on top of me and started punching me in the face, not until he broke my nose and I started bleeding. I fainted, don't know why but maybe because blood makes me nauseous even if it's my own blood. The last thing I could remember chutiya calling me asshole till I lost consciousness.

14. Mazel Tov

I woke up and found myself in a hospital. I could see a bandage down the eye where my nose used to be and apparently felt the need to pee. Chutiya entered and I kind of hated him now. He saw me got up and going towards the bathroom. He came forward to help but I declined it. I don't want help from an asshole who broke my nose. I saw the nurse clearing the bed for me and helped me get back on the bed. She was hot by the way but the moment wasn't right for an erection or masturbation. The pain in the nose was still there. I saw the clock struck 730 and apparent no sunlight suggests its evening. So my Thursday gone just because of a petty fight and I forgot that I was old compared to him and he has still got the power to beat the shit out of me. That was my biggest mistake.

"You okay?" he asked

"Do I fucking look like okay to you?" I gave the same dialogue he used on me

He became silent. Probably understanding that it wasn't a good time to talk.

"Sorry" he said

"Really after you break my nose?"

"It was a moment of passion and you know I have been dealing with things and your way of talking to me just hit the nerve and so…"

Is the fucker asking for forgiveness or just saying to stay away from him

"It won't happen again, I promise"

"Yeah, the next time it happens, I am going to fire your ass"

"Got it, there won't be a next time because I quit" he said and he became serious

What the fuck he was saying?" No man, you can't quit, now who the fuck is going to help me with my story?"

"That's for you to decide"

Shit, is he serious

"How the fuck am I going to decide? You told me to never give up and now you're just doing that. What kind of person are you?"

"Fucked up actually"

"Nah man"

"I guess it's goodbye then"

Damn, didn't really give it a thought that it was going to end like this. I didn't wanted to end this.

"What about drinking together?" I said, hoping he would stop

"Prateek's there" he said while he walked up to the door

"You fucking crazy, I don't even know the guy"

"Hmmm"

"What are you going to do then?"

"I am going back to Pune. Probably do a job or business or whatever. I am sure I will figure it out"

"Okay just listen for one second"

He stopped at the knob of the door

"What"

"What made you decide this?"

"There's nothing left for me here"

"That's life man, you just got to figure it out like you said but not by going back"

"Dude, Mumbai was a disaster but Pune was always ready to embrace me so....good luck"

"You fucker, call me when you get there"

I saw a jittering, that's hesitation. "Yeah I will" he said and smiled and thus went off.

I just couldn't believe the fucking fact that he was seriously leaving. He was stand up guy and I always thought he will remain like that but I guess when times change, people change. Thursday just went like this, the hangover, the fight, the hospital and finally bidding goodbye to my best friend aka chutiya.

Dude, I will never forget you and I am going to fucking kill him if he doesn't call back.

Suddenly out of the blue, tears started rolling down my cheeks.

Really, going to miss you man.

15. All For Family

It was 10 in the morning when I got discharge from the hospital and took the medications from the hospital store. It was bright sunny Friday morning and apparently Mumbai was breathing fresh. I took a cab and reached my apartment. Chutiya already given me back my keys and I assumed that he already might have moved out. I was kind of feeling sorry for the guy because when gives you a sudden jack in the ass, it depends on us whether to stand up or to stand down.

I checked my cell phone and Zerifa called me like 9 times last night. I was going to call her when I saw Rima slowly crying on the stairs leading to my apartment. She was startled by my presence and I sat down beside her, slowly pushing back her hair and clearing her tears. She hugged me, tightly and it was long time since she did that. I was feeling overwhelmed.

"What happened darling?" trying to be as cool as possible

"I am sorry Dad" she said while still crying

"Okay but why?"

"For all the things I said"

"It's okay honey"

"Will you forgive me?"

"Yes darling, I am your Dad and I will always forgive and will be there for you till my last breath"

She hugged me even tighter

"Mom said something today"

"Yes?"

"That she was going to marry again"

What the fuck? Radhika why?

"Why would she say that?" trying to be calm

"She said that she can't be held back anymore as she believes she also has a choice. She's so selfish" she said

"Its okay hon. I am there for you" I said and started massaging her

"I am sorry for what I said earlier and I really want you in my life Dad"

"I want you in my life too"

She smiled and we were having a moment there. I started to remember all the times when me and Rima were together and this was one of the best moments for us which I will ever endure.

"Let's get an ice cream to hit the road" I said as we got up

Why the fuck was she going to marry again? She doesn't even understand the fact that Rima is upset about it.

We stopped at a Mother Diary and ordered for two cones. She was enjoying it and I was enjoying the fact that she was with me.

I dropped her home and thought about to get the stuff I forgot to bring last time I was here. Rima knocked on the door.

She opened and was looking worried "Rima, why did you skip school?"

"None of your business Mom" she said as she went upstairs

"What the hell is wrong with this girl?" she said while looking at me

"I don't know" I said with a little sarcasm

"Why are you here? You are not going to get sex anymore" she said, probably angry at me

"Yeah I know that, I am just here for the stuff that I forgot to take last time" Pointing at the vegetables kept on the table.

"Well thanks to me, I didn't put it on the trash" she said as she went to the kitchen to get the stuff

"Thank you for not putting it in the trash"

She brought back the bag I forgot last time.

"Here" she said

"Thanks" I said

"Where did you find her?" she said as I was about to turn

"Crying in the staircase of my apartment"

"Oh, why?" she was confused

"Because she told me you told her that you're getting married again"

"Yeah, I have to talk to her"

"Yeah, you should because apparently you're the worst mom for her right now"

"Yeah? She said that?"

"Apparently she was cursing you"

"Okay, huh" she said as she was looking at her feet

"What?" I could sense she was trying to say something

"She is doing the same thing"

"What same thing?"

"The same thing she did when you announced that you're going to marry again"

Wow that's a blower. I never thought of the fact she could react to this, I mean she's my daughter but she just reached her teenage years and she has to spend for more than forever trying to get over the estranging hormones which will take over her system eventually.

"She never told me" I said

"Apparently she cried over the fact that we were getting separated and she almost lost herself when she got to know that you're marrying again" she said with utmost polite

I took a deep breath "Never really asked her about this"

"Why do you think she took up smoking" she said with sarcasm

I was defeated to her, getting to know that my daughter almost ruined her life cause of me and that too because of my own selfish happiness. I should have talked to her before taking any decisions. Parents usually don't do that and that's the reason why children tend to get distanced from them and by the time they know, they're already late.

I couldn't say anything but to just look down at the ground and apparently taking off. I couldn't get any more embarrassed. But before that I went up to her room

I knocked at the door as she was checking her cell and apparently wiped her tears upon seeing me.

"Hey you okay?" I asked as I went over to her

"Yeah I'm good" she replied as she smiled

"What?"

"Nothing just…I am happy that you are there for me"

"I always will" I said and hugged her tight "I am sorry by the way"

She got out of my hug and saw me in the eyes "Why?"

"Because I never understood how you'd felt the moment when I announced that I was going to get married again"

"Yeah, I was angry but I don't know, maybe I forgave you" she said and smiled

"I'm glad and I assure you I am not going to make the mistake without asking you first" I said as I brought up her chin and smiled at her eyes. They're damn beautiful

I got up and made myself get out of there with my stuff. I didn't want to face the memories of marrying Mona again on my life. Still, I couldn't believe I fell for that evil bitch. If she wouldn't have got pregnant, my life would have been far great than the way it is of now.

16. Breaking Up

I stopped at a canteen near the highway. I ordered for a tea and I was thinking of the times with Rima and apparently comparing them with one I just had. I love Rima and I love the house and I love everything about it and I love Radhika. Oh my god, I still fucking love her or is it just lust because the sex was great but I need to be sure. My phone started to ring suddenly.

It was Zerifa.

"Hello?" trying to sound as cool as possible

"What the hell, man. A guy go out on a date and when things get pretty damn hot and she takes you back to her place to fuck and then suddenly out of nowhere the guy pulls out just because he couldn't get a boner and the next moment you know, the guy never calls her back. I mean seriously, are you an asshole or are you trying hard to become one" she said with no stopping for a break. Geez,

"I am sorry that I couldn't call you. It's just that there was a lot to take these two days…" I said and left the sentence.

"Meet me now. At the Inox near the central park downtown" she said and hung up. What the hell is wrong with this girl. Damn I couldn't even enjoy the tea. I kick started the bike and it took me about an half to reach the destination.

She was waiting by the cafe coffee day wearing a jeans and half sleeved top which was perfectly suiting on her. She was looking hot and the first thing that came to my mind is to fuck her then and there.

"What took you so long?" she said as she sat on the bike

"What are you doing?" I asked as she made herself comfortable on the bike

"What does it look like?" she said

"Well it looks like as if you're asking for a ride to an old man"

"Seriously just fucking start. We need to talk"

She was pretty damn serious by that sentence. When girls usually say that they need to talk, that means you need to listen to what she says and probably make yourself ready for the outburst of slangs and emotional blackmail she's going to unleash on you.

We went to a day restaurant not far from downtown. We ordered for lunch.

"Okay, say" she said

"Say what?" I asked, confused

"Umm okay let me put it to you-'why the fuck didn't you sleep with me'? she said, looking at me like a hawk

"I couldn't" I said, apparently breaking the eye contact

"Why? cause you couldn't get an erection. Am I not that hot? Don't my boobs turn you on? Don't you like sucking them?" she said and was starting to yell. Few of the heads were turning towards us.

"Behave you" I said with great calm as few of the people were looking at me like I was harassing her.

"No, I won't Mr Siddarth Kumar Banerjee. Not unless you tell me the exact reason on why you never call me, just because I am a Muslim? You're really into shitty religious standards?" she said or I should say pretty much yelled

"Listen up girl. I didn't called you not because you're Muslim or hot, but because my life's fucking falling apart" I screamed at her and apparently we were kicked out and told never to come back

We were looking at each other and she started laughing.

"This all seems funny to you?" I said, turning angry

"Apparently so" she said and kept laughing

It wasn't all funny to me, getting kicked out from a restaurant.

"So your life's falling apart?" she asked

"Yeah"

"Care to tell me?"

"Why would you even care?"

"I don't know cause you might feel better you dumbass"

"My books will turn extinct, my agent left me, I have no family and apparently I think I am going to die soon"

"So what was the problem that night? Because your life was falling apart?"

"No that aint the reason"

"So…your majesty please proceed" she said

"Ummm, I am just curious to the fact that 'why the fuck are you trying on me'?" I said, loud and clear

"Excuse me?" she said and apparently turning angry at the same time

"I mean what the fuck are you doing here? You know there's nothing here so why not stop pretending to each other and let's just face the facts cause it was just a fling for one night and move on." There, I did it. I made myself loud out there that I am the biggest asshole that nobody can ever be.

"So what exactly are you trying to say?"

"Okay, umm, let me put things straight. Why the hell are you trying to hit on a guy who is double your age? I mean you can easily be married off to a well-belonging family and live happily ever after. I mean why you are even considering a guy who will die off by the time you still be having years to live?"

I stopped and was trying to see her reaction. I assumed she got offended as I saw her turn red and angry.

"So you think that I was just playing with you. Is that what you are trying to say here?"

"Aren't you?" I said, I just wanted to end all this shit.

"Okay, alright I thought you're different and the fact about you being an old guy, I liked you from the start and I didn't care that you're 40 or whatever. I checked you first before hitting on you as I saw you safe but apparently you're one insecure fuck and now we're done"

She started to walk away and I wasn't feeling anything from inside me to stop her. I think maybe deep down I wanted her to go away from me. I am a guy who was going to end up alone and devastated so why should I pull an innocent soul along with me. I wasn't exactly feeling anything and mostly this was the time when I go to a bar and start drinking hard till I see the daylights out of me but today wasn't that type of day. I never felt for this girl like I felt for my ex-wives, I mean yeah she was one of the best sex but that doesn't count.

She suddenly faded away from my site and my thoughts. I presumably went back to my place, probably thinking about writing again.

17. Finding New Ways

I was sitting by my laptop, thinking about ways to develop a new character to the story but it wasn't easy because you need to lay down the groundwork before even considering going through with it. I am in a position where Suresh was trying to do something new by starting a business but apparently fails because, because, because, shit I lost it again. I closed down my laptop and thought about how to proceed back to the story. I took a normal 10 minute break from all the work I was doing this Saturday morning. It was usually cloudy and according to weather reports, a rain was likely to hit the city very soon and may lead to flash floods. Floods were common in Mumbai and were the time when people usually take precautions. I didn't need one because I lived in apartment 3 storeys up and therefore I had a less risk of being affected.

This Saturday was usually boring because most of them I usually had with Chutiya smoking weed until dusk. Those were the normal Saturdays for me and everything was so much in place. I felt a big void in my heart and mind as I had nothing to do apart from writing the shitty story about Suresh Yadav finding his true love.

I opened the fridge and took out the last beer can which chutiya brought here. I really missed the guy and the times we were high.

Finishing up the can, I thought about Sanjay and Komal. I couldn't wait till tomorrow to see them as I wanted to see their faces. They were lucky charms for me and so not thinking for a second, I just took off to see them. I don't know what made me but I just can't see the fact that I have to waste another single day to see them and that too for just 2 hours. It took me a while to reach Mona's place and apparently the place was locked.

I was feeling tormented and sad. It was like my world was falling apart and the fact that I couldn't stop it was making me feel sick and annoyed. I felt like killing someone or bomb a city. I punched the door and kicked it, thinking what the fuck happened to my life. I felt like hell and seeing that nobody really cared whether I live or die. I was depressed and angry at myself because it was after all my fault that I didn't write for the past fucking five years and now chutiya is gone. It was me who made the move on Zerifa and realizing that there was something between us, at least chemistry or a connection or whatever.

I felt crap and realizing I had nothing to do, I went over to Blueberry's. Unfortunately, the shop was closed along with my luck.

Seeing nothing left, I went back to my place. I lied on the bed and watched the fan circle around itself.

Realizing I had nothing left, I thought of killing myself and the best option to do was to hang you up the fan. I was thinking of a suicide note as it will be my last writing piece and I wanted it to be perfect. Never realized that I already passed out.

Nostalgia

It was a hot may morning. I was sitting by my laptop and checking my emails for any fan or threat letters. Sanjay was playing with the new console that I bought for him a few days back and Komal was happy with the new lehenga she bought. Mona was in the kitchen, probably making breakfast. I was a little frustrated as I was facing the writer's block now for 3 years. And I was thinking about a way to pay this month's alimony to Radhika. I was out of funds and for the last few months, I was paying through Mona's salary. She wasn't happy but eventually she kind of supported me. Rima hated me from neck to leg and it was almost a year since I last saw her face. I felt like irritation and depression while thinking about all of this. Suddenly I felt a hump on my pants and slowly I got an erection. Didn't know why the hell was I turned on but realized that I needed sex that moment. I titled my head towards the kitchen to check Mona's ass and it made me fucking hard. Pushing the erection into the elasticity of my pants, I went over to the kitchen. She was cutting the onions and I assumed she was kind of in a bad mood. I touched her ass and brushed my penis against it.

"Stop it" she said

I started kissing on her neck and pushing her hair behind her ears. I turned her around and started kissing her. I tried to get my tongue inside her but she was firm.

"Fucking stop it" she sad and pushed me away. I was confused, she never said no when I wanted to have sex.

"What happened babe?" I asked, concerned on whether she was on her period

"Just...today's not a good day"

"Are you?" I asked

"No"

"Then?"

"I don't want to have sex with the kids around"

"That's okay, they're busy with themselves" I said and pressed her boobs

"No, stop it" she pushed me again

I was getting irritated, "Then what the fuck is the problem?"

She was looking me in the eye, probably thinking something deeply. She suddenly came over to me and unhooked my pyjamas.

"You want it?" she started the dirty talk

"Oh yeah" I said, probably excited at the thought of getting a blowjob

"Then you'll get it" she said and went down, pulling my pyjamas and underwear down, she grabbed my penis and started giving me head. Oh, it was fantastic.

I became hard quickly and I pulled her over, turning her around, closing the kitchen door and pulling down her panties. I went inside her. She gave a mild orgasmic sound. I started fucking her and that too using the doggy style position.

"Fuck me like you mean it, Ah" she said

"Oh yeah" I said and pressed her boobs

"Fuck me like it's the last time"

"Oh yeah"

"Fuck me like it's the last time you're going to fuck me"

"Uh-huh"

"Fuck me you motherfucking asshole. Fuck me. Fuck me till you come"

"Oh baby, I want to come inside you"

"Come inside me. I don't care. Just fuck me"

"Oh yeah I'm gonna fuck you"

"Fuck me cause it's the last we're ever gonna fuck"

"Ahhhhh" I said and came inside her. The last time I did that, Sanjay was born

She wore back her panties and adjusted her hair, I wore back my underwear and the pyjamas.

"It's not gonna happen anymore" she said as she was buttoning her top

"What?" I said as I was exhausted

"I said it's not going to happen anymore"

"What's not going to happen anymore?"

"Sex and us"

"What do you mean? What the fuck are you talking about?"

"I mean I want a divorce"

I was shocked that she said that. What the fuck is she thinking?

"What?"

"I thought about it a lot and maybe it's time we both grow up"

"What do you mean by growing up? You just can't decide to divorce and why the hell do you wanna divorce?"

"I don't know. I just want it"

"Don't you love me anymore?"

"Love you? Huh, I stopped loving you the day you made me pregnant and just because of societal pressures, I had to marry you and you're sick old fuck who's gonna die soon anyway and there was fucking future here"

"Are you fucking kidding me?"

"Am I not looking serious?"

Holy motherfucking shit

"I am going to take custody of the kids and if you decide to run the divorce thing smoothly, I will let you meet them twice a week"

"You're not going to take my fucking kids you bitch, you motherfucking bitch" I sad and went t open the door. She tried to stop me and I punched her in response.

I went over to the living room to see the kids. They're so fucking happy in their world and that asshole bitch was going to take them away from me.

I took Sanjay as Komal was checking her lehenga.

"C'mon buddy, we're going on a ride"

"Daddy, where are we going?" he asked

"Someplace happy" I said and took the car keys. I tried to take Komal but by that moment Mona came and stopped me from taking her

"Get out of my way"

"No, no, Siddarth, leave the kids or I will swear to God that I am going to crush you" she said, enmity in her voice.

"Oh yeah, I am going to kill you the next time I saw you" I said and took Sanjay

She stopped me and tried to punch me but she failed, I returned her punch back. We were on each other's hairs, screaming and the kids were crying. All the noise made the neighbours come and break us off. She accused me of harassment and the next moment you know, the cops arrests me andI am under lockup.

By the next morning, I get to know that she has pressed several charges against me, including rape and because our country doesn't give a second thought of verifying the charges, the innocent guys end up in jail.

I was in jail for 1 fucking week.

18. Doing the Chores-1

I wake up from the nightmare from the constant knocking on the door. It was already noon of Sunday. I went over to answer the door and it was Chutiya aka Karan. He was there with a backpack. I hugged him and I could tell he wasn't expecting it.

"What the fuck are you doing? I'm not gay"

"I know you're not you fucker, I am just happy to see you" I said

"I know" he said and we broke into laughter

"How much have you written?"

"Not much man, I just can't write shit"

"So what do you wanna write about?"

"What? You're not going to force me to write this shit anymore?"

"Nah man, I already lost Darshana and I couldn't lose you man. You're my best friend man and every guy needs that"

Wow, that simply touched me heart and made me smile.

"Apparently she didn't deserved you too"

"What do you mean?"

"I mean the night I went out on my date"

"Yeah?"

"I didn't had sex that night"

"What? But you said you had"

"I know. I lied"

"Then what happened?"

"I went over to Darshana"

"What?" he said and standing up

"Sit down fucker. Hear the whole story out"

He sat down

"I went over to her place to make her understand that how great you guys were together"

"And?"

"I saw her with an another guy"

He took a deep breath

"Why didn't you tell me?"

"I thought it might break you as you were facing through a transition"

He calmed down

"That's why I'm happy for you" I said

"Why?"

"I'm happy that you stood up"

He gave a wry smile with a smug on his face.

"I came back because they won't take me back"

Shit

"Why? What happened?"

"They kind of told me to never come back once I made the decision to leave engineering and move to Mumbai"

"Shit man"

"Yeah, but it's okay. I'm good"

I patted his back. I felt he needed that

"You are going through a new story?" he asked

"Nah, I think Suresh Yadav deserves some recognition"

"For?"

"Bringing us together"

We hi-fived and I switched on the laptop.

It took us approximately 5 hours to type 10 pages of shit. We made some rolls and lighted them up. The next moment you know we were high and chutiya started playing 'the real slim shady' on his phone. Takes an Eminem to take us that high.

It wasn't exactly a long Sunday.

19. Doing the Chores-2

I was writing and writing till I stopped to catch a break. I wanted to kill as little time as possible to not get distracted out. Karan was sleeping on the couch and I was thinking of a better possible climax to the story.

Someone suddenly knocked on the door. It was Mona with the kids. The kids came running to hug me and I was like not even brushed yet.

"You didn't came over to see them yesterday, so I brought them over"

Wow, she did a big good deed and that too for me. I was shocked rather than surprised

"Thanks"

"Yes and" she took a moment to check the apartment. "I took the day off just to be with you and the kids"

She suddenly saw chutiya, totally stoned by the last night encounter

She raised her eyebrows as she was giving me the expression that she didn't expect this.

"I am sorry, I didn't expected you to come here"

"Then what did you expected? The kids love you and you're still living like an asshole"

"I know I'm sorry"

"No, I'm sorry" chutiya said "We had a party last night as a reunion party.

"Really?" she said, looking at me and chutiya

"Yeah, I moved out of town a couple of years back and I returned just last night and I kind of pressured him to pass out"

Chutiya was trying to take the whole blame from me. I was kind of glad.

"Okay, well I hope there won't be a next time" she said, probably buying the whole crap

"There won't, I promise" I said with utmost honesty

"Hmm, okay umm let's clean up the place, shall we?"

"Yeah sure" I said

"Good" she said and surprisingly kissed me. That was totally out of the blue.

She went over to the bedroom to clean up as I was busy checking her perfect ass. Chutiya and I, we both were shocked by the spontaneous moment. Shit

"Daddy, we want to help" both of them said together

"No, you two are going to help me with the stuff in the living room. Okay?"

"Okay" they said in unison

It took us nearly 3 hours to clean up the whole goddamn apartment. I was satisfied because the last time I cleaned was the time I bought the apartment.

"There, that should do it" she said with a sigh of relief

"I can' thank you enough" I said and held her hands

"Hmm I'm glad" she said and kissed me. This time a bit longer and she was allowing my tongue inside her mouth.

Chutiya was shocked but the kids were giggling.

We broke off "I'm sorry" I said, don't know why

"It's okay"

"You know I got this thing and umm we need to go" I said, signalling chutiya to get out of here.

"Oh okay umm alright"

"Yeah and we are bit off late" I said, why was I feeling shy. I fucked her for more than 500 times then why the fuck was this happening

"Okay umm then call me later?"

"I can't" I said, I didn't want us back together

"Okay umm you know what, I have to go too"

"Okay"

"C'mon kids, we have to go"

"But I wanna stay with daddy" said Sanjay

"No, your daddy has to go to some WHERE" she said, pressing on the last line

Within a moment, she was gone.

Chutiya and I, both were thinking of the moment but in different terms

"What the fuck just happened" he asked

"I don't fucking know"

"She kissed you" he said

"I know"

"Why the fuck did she kissed you?"

"How the fuck would I know"

"Dafaq you wouldn't know"

"I don't fucking know"

"Shit man" he said as he sat down on the now cleaned couch

"Total shit"

"So what are you gonna do?"

"Do?"

"Yeah like are you going to have sex with her?"

"No man"

"Why not? You know she has the perfect ass"

"That's not the point. I didn't divorced her just to get back with her and she has fucking husband now and I'm not going to have an affair for god's sake"

"Jesus Christ"

We were totally outdone by the things that happened today. I was totally outdone by the things that were happening with me lately.

First Radhika has sex with me and tries to get back together, Second you know chutiya leaves. By the time third comes, I dump Zerifa and chutiya returns back to count four and finally leading to Mona who seduces me just to have an affair. My life was a total soap opera

It was a total crapathon in my head and the only thing that could make me help get out of this is by typing shit and so I went back to my lappy.

I wrote about anything that could come in my head and the next thing you know, I managed to finish up to 50 pages. It was 9 by the time I took a break. Chutiya was watching 'two and a half men' that really made him kill his time.

I went to my bed to get some sleep. One day of cleaning the house and getting the crap inside my head was too much to bear.

20. Time Ends/Deadline

Tuesday and Wednesday went with a flick of an eye. These two days of the final week were so fucking boring that I don't give a damn care to mention. Tuesdays went with sight-seeing as well as checking my facebook page for any fan messaging. These days browsing through facebook leads you to some shitty pics and awful posts. But as because of facebook policy of connecting the world, shitty posts ends up being the most liked ones. Facebook somehow lead me to Google which lead me to Pornhub which lead to my masturbation. It's a good thing because once you realize you're not getting sex from any women, it's time to jerk off. Sometimes I wish I was a porn director but for that I needed to be In the US as our society thinks these practices as illegal. Somehow down the lane, eating chicken mcnuggets and realizing that tomorrow is the D-day as in the day when my publisher is going to kick my ass.

I haven't even gone half way through and the day has come. Time really flies fast. Chutiya has been staying at my place since Sunday and apparently the only thing he is useful is when I needed to go high as he was an expert roll maker and also he could arrange weed and alcohol at the same time with less than two hours. Kind of a talent he's got.

I wake up and see the clock past 9 in the morning. I take a quick bath, probably calling out god's name since I didn't wanted to get fired but still as a matter of fact, I didn't cared much.

I take the car keys

"Wait man, I'm coming with you" chutiya said from the couch, already dressed

"Nah man, I can handle it"

"It's not about handling man" he said while trying to express something

"Then what?"

"I just want to be there for you man and if the bitch fires you, I am quitting too"

"I thought you already did"

"Fuck you. I am just trying to bring out an expression"

"Yeah yeah I got it" I said and went over to hug him. He was my brother from another mother

"Yeah okay, don't be gay about it" he said as he broke off the hug

I lock the apartment and went to the garage to start the car. It was mild Thursday morning and the clock was already going to hit 10. I got heartbeats before starting the engine.

"Don't worry man, I'm with you okay?"

"Yeah" I said as I took a deep breath

We took off and it took us about 2 hours to reach Malabar Hills. I was a little nervous about the whole damn situation we were about to face against that bitch. I checked myself twice before getting out of the ear. I went over to the door as chutiya was following me up.

I straight went to that bitch's office as I didn't wanted to go over the formality of everyone asking about the story. She was wearing a silk satire saree which had a border lining down her navel. Got to admit, she was looking kind of hot.

"Oh, I guess you have a story?" she asked with enough sarcasm to muster up in a sentence

"What if I don't have one?" I said with raised eyebrows, enough to piss her off

"Do I need to call the security?"

"No, apparently because I do have a story"

"Really, wow, thank you sir" she continued, looking at some of the potential investors

"This guy literally took 5 years to write a book. Huh" she said with a smug on her face

All the guys on the table were laughing and staring at me.

"Wasn't the guy won the Pulitzer a few years back?" asked one of them

"Yeah, after that he thinks himself as God, literally" she said and everyone broke into laughter

I checked back to see chutiya but the fucker wasn't there. He was hitting on an intern. So much for brothers.

"So what exactly have you written about? AIDS?" she said and smirked

Fucking bitch "No I. have. written a love story"

"A love story? Really from you?" she said "Fucking shit"

She stood up "Look here people, this guy is a fine example of recession" she said and all the other people broke into laughter

It was crap for me but I had nothing to do but to listen. I wanted this job so I had to compromise.

"What's the love story about?" she asked with another strike of sarcasm

"It's on the flash drive" I said and pulled the USB out of my pocket

"No, I want to listen to prologue from you" she said, raising her eyebrows to the limit

I was not in the mood exactly "Perhaps some other time" I said with my raised eyebrows

"No, I will format the drive and keep it for my personal use if you don't put up a trailer for it right now right here in front of me" she said as she came close to me

I took a deep breath and sighed "Fine" I said slowly

She went back to sit on her chair

"It starts with a guy with Suresh Yadav who falls in love at first sight with a girl named Nisha kandekar. Umm she comes from a high profile society whereas Suresh comes from a poor background. But eventually they both fall for each other and want to get married ASAP. But the only hurdle is her father who will never accept some lame poor guy as his son-in-law. But they managed to..."

"So basically you copied from an old bollywood flick" she snapped, poking at my made up speech

"No no it's not about some bollywood flick. It's about two lovebirds fighting for their love. I even put sex on it"

"Really old man?" she said and everyone broke into laughter "You seriously think I am going to waste my time into it?"

"It's a winner, I can assure you"

"Winner? It's not even the L of LOSER and seriously it's crap"

"But I thought that you wanted something that earns"

She sighed " I wanted you to get out but apparently since you created a scene the last time we met, I gave you a last chance and that too you created a crap"

"I can fix it" I said

"Don't okay. You even called me an evil bitch remember?"

"That was out of passion. I didn't meant it"

"Yes you did"

"Okay but I want to write and I can make it"

"But I don't want you to be here anymore. This whole 2 week was a drama okay? Now I have to go through the formality of kicking your ass out. If you don't mind"

Chutiya suddenly entered.

"Oh look, it's the asshole's partner in crime" she said

"Okay, things didn't work out here" he said

"Work out? What the fuck did your client wrote about?"

"I. don't. know. actually" he said. I was shocked at his statement. He was the motherfucker who gave me whole goddamn idea to write this story

"Well you should read it first" she said

I was fucking angry at the bastard and I couldn't control myself and put myself on him. I punched him again and again till his nose was broken

"You fucking snake. You motherfucking snake"

I kept on punching him and this time I was not letting him getting the advantage. Some of the people broke us off.

"That's enough, both of you" Priyanka said (the publisher)

"I am gonna kill you the next time I see you anywhere I swear to God you asshole son of a bitch"

"Yeah, well I will be waiting for you" he said

I just can't believe he suddenly took a U-turn. The thing kept blowing in my mind

"As for you, get the hell out of there and never show your face here ever or else you're going to jail and this time for sure nobody's going to bail you out" she said, pointing to the fact that she bailed me the last time.

"Screw it" I said and took the flash drive and crushed it. Chuitya was shocked as I destroyed his hp flash drive with a smack.

"I am out of here anyway" I said and took off. I didn't thought twice to look back. Life is full of backstabbers and I realized that I just got set up.

It was devastating and I was depressed. Fucking shit.

My life was a mess, total mess and now I don't have a future, no contract, no agent, no best friend, and no partner. It was like I had no use to be in this world.

I went past through Andheri West and suddenly saw Zerifa's house. I wanted to say her sorry for the fact that because of me she had to go through so many hardships. Sigh

Don't know what happened but I started feeling guilty. I switched off the ignition and went over to her house to apologize. She really deserves that much from my side.

I knock on the door as well as ring on the doorbell. It took her 5 minutes to open

"What do you want?" she said, partially opening the door, implying that she didn't wanted to see me anymore

"I just came here to apologize for my behaviour that day"

"yeah okay" she said and tried slamming the door in my face.

"Wait" I said, trying to stop her "Are you alone?" thinking of the situation of Darshana

"Yeah, why you want to have sex?" she said with a sarcasm "You men are all same. You just want sex"

"No no that's not the point"

"Then what is?"

"I had a similar situation a while back and ended up knowing the secret I never would have wanted to know"

She calmed down

"Are you being honest?"

"Yes, I'm honest"

She saw me from tip to toe " I was having a beer, you want to join?"

"Beer, yeah sure as long it's not hot coffee, eh?"

"You seriously think that you're going to get laid?"

"No, you misinterpreted me. I meant to say that I wasn't in a mood for coffee"

"Really?"

"Yes"

"Okay"

She said as she closed the door.

Life is full of expectations. You never know who to trust and who to believe but you should never lose faith and hope is the best option.

Maybe someday things will turn out…eventually.

As for the time being, I didn't have sex with her but we kind of resumed our friendship. Who knows what it might turn out?

Radhika became my consultant for books as I opened my own publishing house with the small loan that I got from the bank.

Mona was nicer to me and we're having a dynamic friendship. I didn't want to cross beyond that line.

As for chutiya, I never met him again. The last time I heard, he got married to that bitch. Totally matching, ASSHOLE MARRIES THE BITCH.

As for now, I am looking above in the skies. Seeing a falling star and drinking up the beer in the terrace of my apartment and watching a couple having sex.

Life isn't always what you want it to be. It depends on what you actually want your life to turn it out to be.

So I put down the beer on the terrace wall, looked up the sky and saw a star twinkling amidst the cloudy background.

I smiled and the next moment that I couldn't think…

Gravity did her job.

EPILOGUE

After three months

"This prize is because of the many things I had witnessed throughout my life" was my opening sentence at the award ceremony at the Pulitzer prizes in New York City.

It was a room full of hypocrites lying down at their chairs with no remorse, just to show their fake praise for the winner. He hated hypocrites.

After the gala, followed by the buffet of many wonderful dishes lined up. He was very busy with the whole media and the presentations and his post award speech. He was happy, at least he never thought the shitty book that he wrote would ever even make up to bestsellers list was a big achievement. I was feeling very proud of him. Not that I hated him at the time but our marriage was on the rocks. We never talked much because all we did was fucking each other. No love making-just pure hard fuck. It was like I am some kind of bitch he fucks every night. It wasn't pleasant but I had to because he was my husband.

We came back to our room and he was folding his suit. I was changing at the washroom. The room was amazing, I mean top of the world. It had the best facilities available. Sometimes being someone with famous really gives you the credit.

Suddenly he opens the door, sees me half naked and starts pressing my breasts and looks me in the eyes. The next moment you know, his penis is inside me and this time he fucks me rough, very rough and was calling out names like 'bitch come to me, come to me like you mean it'. All I could think was about giving him pleasure. After he comes inside me, he walks away.

I get dressed and went to the room.

"I need a divorce" he says and goes out of the room.

For the first few minutes, I couldn't think and the next I was shocked.

But I wasn't surprised because I knew this was coming but I slugged thinking that he wanted me to get out of his life just the day when he becomes an international star.

My life was about to be shattered and I couldn't do anything about it.

Karma will be back, that's all I could think at that time, crying.

"Do you think that might have caused his death?" asks the therapist

"I don't think so, maybe" said I

"Thank You, Miss Radhika, talk to you soon" said the therapist and shakes my hand

I walk out of her office and go towards my car parked in the lobby. I take one look at the sky, smile at the golden sun. It's a pleasant day.